AD NAUSEUM

13 Tales of Extreme Horror

C. W. LaSART

For Julie,
You are so damned
cute. Love you, Lady!
Carin (C. W. LaSart)

Dark Moon Books

DARK MOON BOOKS
Largo, Florida

AD NAUSEAM

Dark Moon Books
An imprint of Stony Meadow Publishing
3412 Imperial Palm Drive
Largo, FL 33771
Visit our website at www.darkmoonbooks.com

Printed in the United States of America

Cover Artwork: Whendy Muchlis Effendy
Cover Design: Stan Swanson

DEDICATION/ACKNOWLEDGEMENTS

This collection is gratefully dedicated to all of my friends and family. Thank you to Stan Swanson and Dark Moon Books for taking a chance on me, and to Kacy Danek for being my personal coach, friend, and unpaid editor. Last but most certainly not least, thank you to my wonderful parents, precious children and beloved Lou. Without your love and support, I would achieve nothing in this life.

Many thanks as well to the Dark Moon crew including Araminta Star Matthews, Kurt Reichenbaugh and Max Booth III for all their hard work and Whendy Muchlis Effendy for his wonderful cover art.

—C. W. LaSart

CONTENTS

SIMPLE PLEASURES

JIMMY SQUATTED BY THE garden, his elbows resting on dirty knees. He pushed back his ball cap to scratch his receding hairline, squinting in the early morning sunlight at the small pile of gleaming guts in the grass.

Hmmmmph! Now what the hell is that? Though it was only a thought, he still flinched, waiting for Mama to cuff his ear for cursing. Mama had been dead and buried for over a year, but he still felt her presence, hovering in anticipation of his next infraction.

Edna DeLeon hadn't raised her only child to be a foul mouth.

The guts looked clean, not bloody like they'd been torn out by a cat or something. Jimmy thought they probably came from a rabbit or squirrel. A tiny, dark organ that may have been the liver was attached to the innards by a vessel no thicker than a thread. He poked at the pile with his index finger, wondering how it came to be in his yard, and where the rest of the unfortunate critter was. His finger began to tingle and he pulled it back in surprise. There was a faint odor around the pile he hadn't noticed before, not the sort of nasty smell one associated with entrails, but a light, musky odor. It was almost pleasant. Jimmy inhaled deeply to breathe in more of the scent.

As the unusual smell flooded his senses, he regarded the pile of guts with more curiosity than distaste. James DeLeon was a lot of things, but squeamish was never one of them. He grabbed the squishy pile of guts in his bare hand, meaning to throw them on the compost heap at the edge of the garden, but one end of the intestines seemed stuck to the grass. He tugged slightly, the slimy rope stretching a bit before the resistance he felt became a pulling of its own. It slipped through his hand and disappeared into the ground, with a faint slurping noise that reminded him of eating his Mama's spaghetti.

What on Earth?

The entire mess was gone; only a small, irregular hole in the ground marked where it had been. Jimmy blinked. *Had that really just happened? Did the ground really just suck those guts up like pasta?*

His whole hand tingled now and, though it had faded somewhat, the unusual scent lingered. Jimmy leaned forward, his nose pressed to the grass as he peered into the tiny hole left behind. It was hardly bigger than a drinking straw, the edges dark with raw soil. It actually looked like an earthworm burrow. The way the intestines had wriggled out of his hand was certainly worm-like.

Jimmy straightened up and wiped his hands on his overalls before heading down the path to the house. It was awfully warm this morning and he'd been working in the garden for a while. His back was sore from being hunched over so long and he accepted that he wasn't a kid anymore. Maybe he should just go in and have himself a cool glass of water and a short nap. He decided it was a good idea and, resisting the urge to glance back at where the little pile had been, he mounted the steps and entered the house.

He had almost convinced himself the whole thing hadn't happened, or that maybe it had been a big ol' night crawler he'd gotten hold of, but one thing still troubled him. As he went about his daily chores, the same question kept returning to his mind.

Why would a pile of innards, or an earthworm for that matter, have given him half a hard-on?

***

Jimmy suffered fitful dreams that night and woke up early the next morning, feeling tired and a little hung-over.

When Mama had been alive, she never allowed beer in the house. The day he put her in the ground out at Shady Pines Cemetery, Jimmy brought home a twelve-pack and, in the year since, made a habit of keeping beer in the fridge at all times. It was no longer *her* house.

It still looked like her house, the same frilly drapes and matching hand-towels adorned the master bathroom.

He hadn't touched anything in her bedroom. But he considered the place *his* now, to be ruled under *his* rules. The beer was the first change. Jimmy had never lived alone before; never left his mother's nest. Initially, he feared he would be lonely, but found the absence of Mama's constant harping and slapping refreshing. He did miss her cooking, though.

After a long shower (there was no one around to berate him for wasting water), Jimmy got dressed and checked the beer situation in the fridge.

Uh oh. Only two left. He decided to go into town. He thought maybe he'd stop by the café for breakfast and see Charlene. Though being in town caused him anxiety, he would do anything for the chance to exchange a few words with his favorite waitress. The thought of seeing Charlene's smile (even if it *was* because she kind of had to) made up his mind. Grabbing his sweat-stained ball cap, Jimmy crammed it on his head to cover his bald spot and headed out the door.

The garage sat at the end of the walk, beyond the vegetable garden. Jimmy stopped abruptly, the sweat on his body cold despite the heat of the late June morning. The pile of guts was back, this time larger than before. Today it looked to have come from a cat or full grown rabbit. The smell was back too, much stronger this time. Jimmy could smell it from ten feet away, and became instantly erect.

4 | Ad Nauseam

All thoughts of beer and Charlene disappeared as he once again knelt in the grass.

The guts felt warm and sticky, once again clean of blood. He hefted them in his hand, careful not to pull at the section that disappeared into the ground like some strange umbilicus. A pleasant tingling permeated his flesh.

"What the blue hell is going on here?" This time Jimmy didn't flinch, ignoring his mother's voice in his head as she berated him for cursing.

James Allen DeLeon! You will not cuss in my house!

"I'm not in the house, Mama. And you're dead."

At the sound of his voice arguing with his imagination, the guts once again *slurped* into the ground. Jimmy grabbed tight to the end, but it broke off in his hand, leaving him holding a scant inch of gleaming intestine. He wiped it on his jeans without thought, his eyes on the hole left behind.

It was larger this time, big enough to admit his sausage-like index finger. Before he could lose his nerve, he poked the finger in and wriggled it around inside the hole. The interior was warm and moist. And *slimy*. Again he thought of an earthworm. Strange. Just as he was about to pull his finger out, the hole began to move. Pulling gently at his finger, it began to make those slurping noises. *Sucking* noises.

Jimmy pulled back so violently that he fell onto his ass in the garden. A tomato plant broke his fall, the fruit squishing beneath his considerable weight and soaking through his jeans.

Great! Just Great! Now it's gonna look like I got my period! He laughed despite himself. Edna DeLeon hadn't allowed cursing in her house, but it was *really* forbidden for men to talk about lady stuff.

Jimmy sat on the remains of the tomato plant, staring at the grass. The dark hole in the ground stared back at him, exuding its seductive odor. He wondered where it had come from and what had caused it.

Should I call someone?

Who would I even call?

He had no family left; his Dad had run off with a cocktail

waitress shortly before he was born, and his mother had been an only child. He had no friends, and never held a job aside from repairing fencing for the farmers down the road. He and Mama hadn't required much money to live on, and she had inherited a tidy sum in her bank account, including the house, when her own folks died. Now that bank account, like the house, was his. His decisions and his *life* were now his own, as well.

When he was still in his twenties, Jimmy had mentioned to Mama that maybe he ought to date girls, like the rest of the guys in town did. Mama quickly squashed that ambition, reminding him how cruel the kids, especially the *girls* at school had been. Mama always said he'd been born with more heart than brains, and she fostered his shyness, not wanting to let anyone be in the position to hurt her only child.

At thirty-seven, James DeLeon hadn't dated since high school. Even then it had only been a few times. Both girls were so shy and sweet that he had been afraid to bring them home to his Mama, worried that she would hurt their feelings. He didn't know if he *could* date at this point, or if he even wanted to. He didn't know how to even start.

Jimmy got to his feet and brushed off the back of his pants. No good. He was going to have to change. Another shower probably wouldn't hurt, either.

The hole in the ground remained, innocuous in the morning light, no outward evidence of the digestive remains it had gobbled up moments before. He once again wondered if there was someone he could tell about the phenomenon, but could think of no one, and walked into the house to clean up.

***

A cheerful bell announced Jimmy's arrival as he entered the diner, closer to lunch time now, since he had showered and changed. There were quite a few patrons, including a couple who occupied his usual corner table. Jimmy took a seat at the counter, disappointed his comfort zone had been invaded. Jimmy nodded at Sam as he walked over in his usual stained apron, looking bored, and laid a laminated menu on the counter in front of him. Charlene only waited on tables, and sitting at the counter made Jimmy the cook's responsibility. He looked over at *his* table in hopes the couple might be finishing up, but Charlene was just delivering their food.

Jimmy really wanted a beer, but ordered a cup of black coffee instead while looking at the menu. Someone pinched the back of his arm, startling him from his sullen inspection.

"Hey there Jimmy." Charlene stood at his elbow, holding three empty coffee cups by the handles expertly in one hand. Her smile, beautiful as always, made his heart skip.

"Uh, hi, Charlene." Jimmy felt himself blush, and tried to stop, only making the heat in his face worse.

"Sorry about the table, Hon. If I'd known you were coming, I would've saved it for ya."

"That's okay. I don't need that table. I was planning on sitting at the counter today anyways." *God, I always sound like an idiot when I try to talk to her!* Jimmy wished he could just slither out the door.

Charlene cocked her head to one side and smiled, clearly amused by his awkward behavior. Before she could reply, a woman across the restaurant called out, her hand waving frantically in the air.

"*Waitress!* Can I have my bill? I'm late for a meeting!" Jimmy thought the woman was rude, and hated her for interrupting their conversation.

"Just a minute," Charlene called back.

She reached out to grab Jimmy's elbow gently, the feel of her hand reminding him of the tingly feeling he got from the hole. He tore his mind away from the memory just in time to catch what she said to him. "I go on break in about forty-five minutes. Would you be able to hang around that long? There's something I wanna ask you."

"Sure!" He said too quickly. "I mean . . . um . . . of course. I haven't even ordered yet. Was thinking maybe a hoagie, or a French dip—"

She smiled at him as the woman needing her bill began to

holler again. Charlene hurried away and called over her shoulder. "Talk to ya in a bit, Jimmy!"

As if on cue, Sam came over with his pad and stood in front of Jimmy expectantly, not saying a word. Jimmy asked for the first thing on the menu, which happened to be a Rueben and fries. He didn't like sauerkraut, but at the moment didn't care. His mind whirled.

What could Charlene want to ask me? What if she was going to ask him to quit coming in on her shifts? What if she thought he was creepy? Jimmy squashed the thoughts before they could blossom into a full blown panic. She probably needed someone to a repair a fence for her Mama. Or maybe for a new *boyfriend?!*

Oh geez! Here we go again!

The next forty-five minutes were the longest in his life, but Jimmy managed to eat his lunch, shoving the sandwich in without thought, and was surprised when it was gone. He almost left then, but suddenly the lady herself slid into the seat beside him, a diet coke in one hand and a pack of cigarettes in the other.

"Whew! What a day! I think everyone must be crabby today. I swear if one more person complains about their food or the bill—she stopped abruptly, her big blue eyes bright with mirth. "Say Jimmy, would you mind talking outside? I only get fifteen minutes and I'm *dying* for a smoke."

Jimmy smiled in his awkward way and nodded. He always found it very charming how she spoke so fast and never seemed to run out of things to say. Charlene made him almost dizzy with her constant chatter, but he liked it. She never seemed self-conscious. He followed her out into the humid afternoon, the bell over the door sounding as they left.

Charlene looked the same as always. *Beautiful.* She kept her blonde hair pulled back in a ponytail, and wore pink eye shadow and lip gloss that matched her uniform. Her skirt was short and tight, giving Jimmy a glimpse of long, tan legs that made him feel slightly lightheaded. She lit a cigarette and leaned against the brick wall, dragging deeply and squinting across the street at their reflections in the shop windows. As an afterthought, she held the pack of smokes towards him.

"Want one?"

"No, thank you." He almost added *Mama wouldn't like that*, but had enough sense to realize this wasn't the sort of thing a grown man should say. Then he glanced at her legs and the roaring blush was back.

"So anyway, I was thinking," Charlene looked away as she spoke, paying too much attention to her cigarette. "There's this picnic on Sunday after service, and I was thinking about going. But with me being divorced for so long and never showing up with a date to anything . . . I know those old women always have their tongues wagging and they have to be saying I'm some sort of lesbian or something."

He knew what a lesbian was, but he was unsure about the mechanics of such a relationship, so he nodded in a way he hoped looked knowing, saying nothing. Charlene stared at him for a minute, her eyebrows raised in expectation, before she finally spoke again, huffing in exasperation.

"I was wondering if you would like to go with me."

"Go with, um, you?" Jimmy felt dizzy. Was she asking him *out?* "Like a *date?*"

"Yeah. Sure. A date." Charlene looked doubtful now and Jimmy felt that familiar panic well up inside him. She might be changing her mind.

"Yes! Sure I would!" Jimmy beamed but she looked unsure, so he toned it down a notch, hoping he appeared less eager. "I mean, yeah. I would go with you."

Charlene smiled then, her teeth uneven and yellowed from nicotine, but still the most beautiful smile he had ever seen. She took out her order book and scratched something on it with her pen, before ripping the sheet off and handing it to him.

"Here's my number, Hon. Call me tomorrow night. We'll figure it out." She crushed the cigarette under her shoe then, with a wink, turned on her heel and left Jimmy to watch her hips swing as she walked back through the door.

He stood there for a moment dumbfounded. *He had a date!* It was too much for him to process. Instead, he tried to remember if he had paid Sam for his sandwich or not. Checking the remaining cash in his pocket, Jimmy got into the truck and headed for the liquor store across town.

***

Jimmy barely heard the liquor store's little bell above the door. He walked to the back of the store and opened the cooler, locating his favorite brand of beer. There was a sale on cases, so he grabbed one instead of the usual twelve-pack. He heard Mama's voice sound off in the back of his head, saying something about an alcoholic, but he ignored her. He was too happy about his date. Mama would have plenty to say about *that* too.

On the way to the counter, Jimmy's eyes fell on the magazine rack in the corner and he stopped. Unlike the racks in other stores, the front was higher so you couldn't see the covers, only the very top where the name was. The beer wasn't the *only* change in the house since Mama had died. He didn't have very many of these magazines, but had collected a few.

He looked at the rack longingly, trying to decide if the embarrassment of purchasing them would be worth the excitement of having some new *material* for his fantasies. He decided he wanted them and grabbed two without even looking to see what they were.

At the register, a kid who looked barely old enough to drink rang up the case of beer, and then stopped with his hand on the nudie mags. He looked around suspiciously, leaning over the counter until he was a little too close for Jimmy's comfort. Then he spoke in a hushed and secretive voice.

"You don't want *these*, man."

Jimmy was flooded with embarrassment, wishing he hadn't grabbed the books at all. A big breasted blonde mocked him from the cover, one hand holding up her breast like an offering, the other hidden in the mystery between her legs. Jimmy looked away, ready to pay for the beer and abandon the magazines.

"I got something better than this shit." The young man smiled and winked. He looked around one more time for good measure, reached beneath the counter, and came up with a shoe box held together with masking tape. "Check these out, man."

Inside the shoebox were DVDs, their covers depicting scenes much worse than any Jimmy had ever seen in his magazines. His heart raced at the thought of *watching* naughty things instead of just looking at glossy pictures, but the excitement quickly waned.

"I don't have a way to play them. Just a VCR."

The kid made a noise of derision and shook his head, placing the box back under the counter and coming up with a larger one. "That's dinosaur shit, pops. But I do have some VHS. Now what you want? Gang bang? Anal? Fetish? Lesbian?"

"Lesbian." Jimmy said quickly, surprising himself. "And, um, whatever else you think is good."

The cashier made a show of digging through the box and inspecting each one, before setting three aside and returning the others to their hiding place. He put money in the register for the beer, but the crumpled twenty for the videos went directly into his pocket. He smiled at Jimmy in a creepy way that made him want out of the store as soon as possible, putting the movies into a paper bag.

"You have a nice day, man. Let me know what you think. If those don't get you off, nothing will!"

Jimmy grabbed the beer and the bag and left without a word.

***

The phone rang ten times when Jimmy finally gave up. Charlene told him to call her *tomorrow* night, but he was too excited to wait. He managed to hold off until after dinner, but spent the entire time staring at the old phone where it sat on the kitchen counter.

Scenarios played through his head. What if she had gotten into an accident on the way home from work? What if she fell and was lying on the floor only inches away from the phone, suffering some terrible injury and forced to listen to the telephone taunting her with its every ring? Or worse! What if she was in her bedroom romancing with some other guy?! The possibilities were endless.

What he really wanted to do was drive straight to town and find out why she wouldn't answer the phone, but didn't know exactly where she lived. He also realized somewhere deep down that this would not be normal behavior. He wanted to be cool with Charlene. *Act cool.* It became his mantra.

Jimmy popped the tab on a beer and began to wash the dishes. Edna DeLeon hadn't approved of a lot of things, and automatic dishwashers were one of them. *Real women,* she told her son often, *didn't need a machine to do their jobs. No machine could ever get the dishes as clean as good ol' elbow grease.*

He was coming to hate his Mama. At times he fantasized about hopping in the truck late at night and driving out to that cemetery to piss on her grave. It would be *beer piss* too! Sometimes these thoughts caused him guilt, but as time passed, the thoughts increased in frequency and the guilt diminished. As he finished the chore, his eyes fell upon the paper bag on the counter.

Jimmy picked up the bag with the intention of stashing the movies in a drawer, certain that he wasn't ready to watch them. But he found himself taking them out of the bag and inspecting each one.

The covers depicted things that would've made his Mama turn over in her grave; the backs had paragraphs describing what each video promised to show him. The language was colorful and foul. Most of the words he didn't completely understand, but having made it half way through high school, he'd been exposed to enough teenage guy-talk to get the gist of it. He grabbed two more beers, drinking one in a single gulp. Just the thought of actually watching the movies made his hands sweat and his heart race. He felt such a bittersweet mixture of excitement, disgust, embarrassment and arousal.

As he grabbed another beer and slid the first video into the VCR, his Mama's voice came again. Jimmy wasn't crazy. He knew her voice wasn't real, but she was there none the less, babbling with rage. *Oh no you DON'T James Allen DeLeon! My own son, a drunken whoremaster! Not in MY house!*

"Shut up, Mama." He said, sitting on the worn couch and pressing play.

His eyes went round and his jaw slack as the images began to grind upon the television screen without any beginning credits. There was no plot whatsoever, no pretense at acting; just raw footage of men and women at their most perverse and primal. Jimmy loved it.

Two hours and countless beers later, Jimmy was just starting the third video. He had masturbated until he no longer could, the beer and his exertions leaving him weak and tired, but still he watched, his gaze riveted onto the screen. Somewhere in the night, an animal wailed in pain and terror, but he paid it no heed.

James Allen DeLeon was learning the erotic details of a lesbian relationship, in living color.

***

When Jimmy awoke in the morning, his head was pounding almost as hard as his heart. He had been in the middle of a graphically erotic dream turned nightmare. In his dream, he was one of the guys in the video, doing nasty things to women, but when he looked up, all of them wore his Mama's face. He sat up fast in bed; his throbbing head making him regret the decision instantly. He felt dirty and hung-over.

And oddly satisfied.

After a hot shower and a hearty breakfast of eggs and hash browns, Jimmy began to feel human again. A couple of aspirin washed down with half a gallon of water restored him to his previously joyful mood from the day before.

I have a date with Charlene tomorrow! He wondered if she had ever done any of the things he had seen on the videos. Just the thought made him blush, but he felt as much excitement as embarrassment. Putting on his cap to shield his thinning hair and scalp from the sun, Jimmy whistled as he headed out back to the garden for his morning chores. He wasn't surprised to see the mess that waited for him.

Pile of guts? *Yep.*

Larger than yesterday? *Sure was.*

He vaguely remembered hearing howling the night before. This time it was a dog, no question about it. A worn collar with no tags lay on the ground beside the innards. He didn't recognize the thing, but it didn't matter anyway. He wouldn't have driven the mile to the nearest neighbor's house just to tell them their dog had been eaten by a hole in his yard. People already thought he was simple. He wasn't about to make them think he was crazy, too.

Jimmy didn't bother handling the guts this time, but he did retrieve the collar and toss it in the garbage can. When he returned and the slimy pile of intestines still lay there, he stomped his foot next to the hole. Sure enough, the guts disappeared in a flash. It left a larger hole behind, and the phantom fragrance that now made him uncomfortably hard after the evening's exploits. Jimmy walked away to tend his garden.

After the gardening, Jimmy spent the better part of the day cleaning house. He didn't know if Charlene would want to come home with him, or if he would even summon the courage to ask, but wanted to be prepared just in case. Hours of scrubbing and dusting chased away his hangover and left him spent but happy. He thought about having a beer for a reward, but then he remembered. Charlene wanted to go to a church function, and though he might do things just to irritate his mother's specter, he certainly didn't want to show up at a social hung-over. He had a feeling that one beer would end up being several.

The phone only rang twice before Charlene answered with her usual cheery demeanor. Jimmy found it much easier to speak to her on the phone. He actually felt *cool* as they chatted and made plans to meet at the picnic the following day. After a half an hour, Charlene said she needed to go and they exchanged their goodbyes, with promises of seeing one another soon. Jimmy fell into bed with a smile on his face.

He awoke around midnight feeling uneasy. It was hotter than hell in his little bedroom and the electric fan by the window pulled in humid air. He was also aroused to a painful degree, sporting the most impressive erection of his life. He lay there for a while; his mind foggy as he tried to determine what had disturbed his sleep. Though he had abstained from drinking that evening, he felt drunk and confused. Another warm breeze blew across his body and he noticed the smell. It was the odor from that hole, only strong enough that he could now smell it in the house. He *felt* it coating his body, teasing him with need.

I wonder if the hole uses that smell to attract its prey. As quickly as this thought came, it was gone.

Still uncomfortably erect, Jimmy formed a fantasy in his mind about Charlene. He blended the scenes from the videos with her face, imagining her taking him in her mouth like those actresses had, willingly, eagerly.

Her mouth. His mind skipped to the day before, the feeling of the hole tightening around his finger, tingling, *sucking* at his finger. He tried to push it away, but then his Mama crept in, her voice disgusted and scornful.

Figures you'd turn out like him. All you men are the same. Just like your Daddy, only worried about getting some whore to play with your worm! Worm. He thought of the hole again, his mind pleasantly fuzzy. The hole. The tingly, sucking hole. The women on the video, sucking shiny purple penises into their crimson mouths. Did it tingle? From the looks on the men's faces, he thought it just might.

Jimmy was out the back door and on the porch steps before he even realized he'd left his bed. The hot night air caressed his body where he stood, wearing nothing more than thin boxer shorts. He couldn't see the hole yet, but the odor was strong, drifting over to him in almost tangible waves, luring him on. He should've been afraid. The piles of guts should've been warning enough to stay away. Jimmy moved as if in an intoxicating dream. He *told* himself it was a dream. Nothing could hurt him while he slept.

Jimmy dropped his boxers and sank down to his knees. Locating the hole with his hand, he could feel its slickness, ready for him like the ladies on the television. On hands and knees he eased forward, plunging himself into the warm, wet earth. The hole began to suck immediately, causing him to cry out with pleasure. The tingling felt so intense that it became almost painful. He bucked and shuddered as the ground tightened and pulled at him, his climax coming hard and fast, but still it went on.

Over and over he found completion, but still the hole sucked at him, the pressure changing from ecstasy to pain, then agony in a second. He cried out and tried to pull back, his limbs weak and worthless. Laying prone on the ground for what felt like hours and unable to struggle, Jimmy screamed his lungs raw, aware in one small, sane portion of his mind that this was no dream and his nearest neighbors were too far away to hear him.

Jimmy heard the smooching sounds of his body being sucked into the ground, inch by inch. His bones cracked like kindling. Electric fire coursed through his veins as his insides turned to liquid and were steadily consumed. Then his spine gave way in one brilliant flare of hot pain before he blessedly lost sensation in his body. His fragmenting mind conjured up the image of an insect, injecting its victim with paralyzing enzymes before slurping up the soupy insides left behind. He clearly heard a sound like a straw at the bottom of a milkshake, sucking up that last little bit of ice cream with noisy enthusiasm.

The last thing Jimmy heard, before the darkness claimed him for its own, was the phantom sound of his Mama's voice.

Filthy, drunken whoremonger! I always knew you were a dirty, stupid boy!

***

Charlene had built up quite a head of steam on her way to Jimmy's place, and by the time she pulled into the driveway next to his beat up old truck, she was more than ready to give him a piece of her mind. She'd been stood up by a lot of guys in the past, but this really took the cake.

I've been stood up by the goddamned village Idiot! Jimmy had been mooning over her for the last year, practically drooling every time he got a glimpse of her ass or down her shirt, and he had the *nerve* to leave her at the damn picnic alone! The only reason she had even considered him was because she needed a date and he seemed nice, if a little slow. He was also kind of cute in a devoted puppy sort of way. She stomped around the garage, her hands balled into fists, sweat from the hot afternoon collecting in the small of her back and under her breasts.

Slowing as the smell hit her, Charlene stopped and looked around. It smelled like sex, heavy and musky. It seemed to come from near the little vegetable garden Jimmy obviously spent much time in. Wrinkling her nose against the odor, she felt an electric jolt of arousal that started in her chest and shot like lightning to her groin. Charlene gasped aloud at the power of the sensation, her gaze falling upon something gleaming in the sun several yards away. Sweating profusely and taking small sips of air, Charlene approached the mound. The throbbing between her thighs was so deep that she ached to press herself against something, a fence post, *anything,* to relieve it.

A stained pair of men's boxers lay crumpled on the ground, next to a pile of intestines. Part of a pale organ, heavily veined in blue, protruded from a hole in the ground that was easily the size of her thigh. Alarmed, but still painfully aroused, and now starting to feel light headed, Charlene inspected the heap of guts, nudging it with her foot, unmindful of the fact that she wore only a pair of flip-flops. Her mouth opened in an *ooooh!* of surprise.

Charlene's foot began to *tingle.*

WIDOW

*D*ANG IT!

Susan swatted the back of her neck, responding to the sudden, searing pain. Her hand squashed something crunchy and soft. Sticky guts squirted between her fingers, causing her stomach to lurch. She slowly brought her hand up before her eyes.

Not a spider, anything but a spider, she thought.

She examined the crumpled black body and green gobs of insides stuck to her fingers. It was indeed a spider. Susan shuddered, repeatedly wiping her hand on a cardboard box to remove the mess.

The back of her neck still stinging, Susan slumped onto a nearby box. Tears filled her eyes.

I can't even clean the basement without drama! she thought. *Oh how Bill would chuckle at me if he could see this, crying over a spider bite.*

Waves of revulsion and self-pity sent shivers through her body. Bill didn't understand. He would never *get it.* He wasn't a mother.

"It's a clear cut case of Empty Nest Syndrome." Bill had asserted in a smug tone that made Susan want to kick him in the shin. He'd been the first to notice the signs of depression as they had taken their toll on Susan, and he was quick to diagnose, as well. "You should find a hobby."

For over twenty years, Susan had dedicated her life to the raising of their two children. Bill made enough money for her to stay home. Twenty-two years of cooking for, cleaning up after, and doing laundry for those children. Soccer games and dance classes, parent teacher conferences and school performances. She had wiped every nose, every tear, and their little butts when they were babies. Broken bones, first periods, first dates and first broken hearts had all been her domain.

Bill had dealt with none of it.

Their youngest daughter had followed in her sister's footsteps and left for college a few months ago, leaving Susan with nothing to do and too much time on her hands. The big house and all its silence echoed faintly with memories. Her kids had been her whole life, and now she felt as empty as the house. She had nothing.

No *purpose.*

It became her mission. *What will you do with yourself today, Susan? What is your purpose?*

Bill had his *purpose* in every day life. Oh, sure he did. He had his job to go to five days a week with meetings and phone conversations. He had his football games on the weekends, which he watched while propped in his armchair relaxing after such a hard work week. He had his drinking as well, empty beer bottles and the occasional pint of hard stuff taking up more space in the garbage can lately. Of course, he also had that little slut at the office. The one he had been having an affair with for years.

Susan had known for a while now. The many nights that he worked late, only to come home smelling of perfume. Credit card receipts for mystery gifts that had never shown up under the Christmas tree. She hadn't considered divorcing him. The embarrassment for both her and the girls would be too much to bear; besides, she was comfortable where she was.

She had everything she could possibly want, except a *purpose.*

***

Bill lay snoring next to her when Susan awoke late in the night, her body soaked in sweat and wracked with chills. Her head pounded fiercely and waves of fever washed over her. The muscles spasmed in her neck, clenching into knots, as she scurried to the bathroom. She barely made it in time before heaving her dinner into the toilet, then further suffering an attack of diarrhea like she had never known.

Please let me die, she thought as she sat on the pot with her face in the garbage can, losing fluids from both ends simultaneously.

After several minutes, the vomiting seemed to subside and there was nothing left within her to excrete, so Susan drew a warm bath. Weak and thoroughly spent, she climbed over the edge of the antique, claw-foot tub into the tepid water and settled in slowly. When the back of her neck touched the edge of the tub, she sat back up with a gasp.

Ouch!

Susan fingered the tender lump on her neck. The spider bite had swollen into a large, hard boil, throbbing beneath the skin. Careful not to slip, she got out of the tub and found her makeup mirror. Angling it so she could see her back reflected in the larger one above the sink, she examined the lump. It was an angry red around the edges, with a head of festering puss that looked as though it may burst at any moment, the skin stretched thin like the surface of an overinflated balloon.

Hmmmm, Susan thought. *All this from a silly spider bite? I think I'm going to have to get this looked at by a doctor in the morning.*

Some time during the early hours of morning, the boil on Susan's neck burst, leaking foul yellow pus onto the ivory sheets. As the wound oozed, her fever broke and she traded in the fitful slumber of illness for a much more restful sleep.

***

Susan slept through the rustling of the sheets and the sound of Bill's electric razor as he started his morning. She even slept through a full hour of her alarm's blare later, before it finally gave up and shut itself off. It wasn't until after lunch that Susan awoke, feeling, not groggy, but as refreshed as if she had just returned home from a long trip to the spa.

Her depression seemed to have lifted, as well. With a renewed energy and vitality that she hadn't felt since her twenties, she got out of bed humming the tune of *Whistle While You Work*, a song from her daughter's childhood that she hadn't thought about in years, as she tucked the sheet corners under the mattress and smoothed the rumples in the blankets on the bed. And best of all, the pain her neck was gone.

Susan attacked the house with manic energy, cleaning and cooking at an almost frenzied pace. She busied herself with chores that she had put off for too long, things that weren't part of her every week routine such as washing curtains and organizing closets. Then she baked muffins and cookies and breads, enjoying the task more than caring who would eat them. She felt a satisfaction in the work that had been missing for some time.

When Bill returned from work, late that evening, she met him at the door eagerly.

Ha! Work indeed! she thought, as she caught the scent of soap on his skin. She could detect the musk of another woman as well. It was faint, but she could still smell it, and she felt her anger glow hot. She hadn't cared about the affairs for a long time now, but tonight she wanted to rip his head off.

Bill stopped short when he saw the fury in her eyes. "What's going on, Hon?"

"Nothing. Nothing at all." Susan forced a civil tone and tight smile. "I made your favorite dinner, stroganoff. Hurry, it's getting cold."

Dinner was a quiet affair, Bill complimenting Susan on a delicious meal, while she stared back across the table, her look inscrutable. Her appetite was gone. Come to think of it, she hadn't eaten anything all day. It was of no concern, she wasn't even hungry. Susan stood to clear the table and load the dishwasher.

"Good Christ Susan! What happened to your neck?" Bill grabbed her shoulder and leaned in for a closer look.

Susan clapped a hand across the wound. "Nothing. It's just a spider bite, that's all." She turned so he couldn't see. "It doesn't even hurt anymore."

"Well, you need to go to a doctor tomorrow. It looks awful!"

Susan knew Bill was right; but, she wouldn't be going to see any doctor. For reasons she couldn't explain, she felt oddly defensive of her spider bite. She should've been more disturbed by the fact that the crater had doubled in size, now big enough to admit the tip of her pinky finger, its edges grey and withered. But the flesh around it had turned a mottled black and green that she found strangely beautiful.

"All right," she said at last, humoring him. "I'll call first thing in the morning."

***

The next day Susan ate a fly.

One moment, it was just flying around, and the next it was crunching between her teeth, bitter guts bursting on her tongue. She hadn't even realized her own intentions when she plucked it out of the air and popped it into her mouth. She waited in horror for the nausea to come, but it never did. Instead, to her amazement, her stomach growled and her appetite returned with a vengeance.

What at odd development, she thought, though she felt no real alarm. Indeed, her nerves seemed more steady with every hour that ticked by. So what if she had enjoyed eating the fly. Many cultures ate insects as a staple of their diet. She had read about African villages where kids carried around enormous roasted grasshoppers on sticks, licking and crunching them like lollipops. She spent much of the remainder of that afternoon hunting and consuming bugs with the same vigor that she had cleaned the house the day before.

She searched every corner of the house for insects, looking in all of the dark places that they liked to hide, even eating the dusty remains of long-dead moths, littering the window-sills. The dead ones were tasteless, but fresh moths had a wonderful plumpness to them, their guts sweet and gritty in her mouth.

The next day, some of Susan's teeth fell out. Just the top canines, but it was still a bit frightening at first. They came out bloodless, replaced by sharp, dark fangs curving out from her gums, which excited her for reasons she still didn't understand. She found that if she concentrated really hard, she could make a clear fluid shoot out of them. When she bit her tongue, it went numb and functionless for over an hour.

Fascinating!

The changes came fast over the next few weeks, but Susan was able to hide them from Bill with ease. He was spending more time at work everyday, and though they still slept in the same bed, they no longer made love. This absence of intimacy allowed Susan to hide the changes to her body by sleeping in her housecoat. She grew more detached from her old life as the days passed. She found herself hurrying off the phone whenever one of her daughters would call. Only a few short weeks ago these same calls would have been the highlight of her day.

Susan knew she should be afraid of the changes, should be seeking help for the uncontrollable shift in her nature, but she had a hard time feeling anything but joy and excitement. The sheer exhilaration that she felt overshadowed the lesser feelings of anxiety and concern. A curious detachment, supplementing the joy, made it impossible for her to worry about such things.

She found she just couldn't be bothered by the more mundane aspects of life. All Susan wanted to do was lay in the empty tub, naked, and stroke her changing abdomen, giddy with excitement when she first felt the hard ridges wriggling beneath the skin, waiting to emerge. The foreign parts hiding beneath the surface of her skin, felt sharp and restless, eager to complete the metamorphosis. Her skin was becoming transparent, allowing hints of black to show through as the appendages pressed against her flesh from the inside.

Her new legs emerged early one evening. The skin of her abdomen had stretched tight and shiny, before it split with a sound like cloth tearing. It was extremely painful, but Susan was brave, clenching her teeth as well as she could around the oversized fangs in her mouth. She barely made a sound as each pair of black, chitinous legs erupted from her sides. There was no blood, only shriveled flaps of white skin left hanging like streamers.

She was becoming complete. She knew the transformation was almost at an end. She felt it in some primitive part of her brain that had been dormant before.

Yes! So close!

The pieces of the puzzle were falling into place nicely, and she could almost see the complete picture. Almost knew what it was that she had to do. Susan pulled an armchair into a shadowy corner of the living room and waited patiently for her husband to return.

Bill staggered in the house, well after midnight, smelling strongly of liquor and sex; he hadn't even bothered to shower this time. Hearing her heavy breathing, he turned towards the corner where she sat, unable to make out more than her shape in the gloom. She looked different, her figure not the soft matronly one that he had gotten used to over the last many years.

Bill felt apprehensive, but he dismissed it. It was just poor, sweet, dumpy Susan. Nothing to be scared of.

"Everything okay, Babe?" His speech was slurred and unsteady.

When she spoke, her voice was strange. A small amount of light from the kitchen pierced the darkness of the room, reflecting off glittery black eyes that seemed both too small and too bright to belong to his wife.

Fear turned knots in Bill's stomach as he tried to push it down.

"Go to bed you cheating son of a bitch."

The accusation startled Bill. He opened his mouth to deny it, and then slammed it shut when he thought about how alien her voice sounded. His usually humble wife had never spoken to him like that. He always suspected that she knew about his infidelity, but just ignored it. He was also certain that she would rather die than bring about that sort of embarrassment on their daughters and extended families. She had been behaving so oddly over the last few days. Tomorrow he would call someone. Clearly, Susan needed help. Though he wasn't the sort of man that allowed his wife to order him around, Bill was afraid. Something was very wrong with Susan, and he wasn't sure he was prepared to deal with it tonight. He quietly went to bed.

Susan waited until she was sure that Bill was asleep, then crept into their room and lay on the bed beside her husband. Her new legs were not yet fully grown, and she was still able to hide them beneath the robe, but her rage was a different matter entirely.

She lay there, listening to him snore loudly, her anger swelling with each noisy inhale and exhale. His snoring was always at its worst when he drank, and tonight was no exception. She allowed her rage to build until she could stand it no longer. For too many years she had lain beside this man, faithful when he was not, caring when he was indifferent, loving when he was undeserving. Tonight he would get his. She would give him everything he deserved.

With a speed she hadn't known she possessed, Susan flung off her robe and jumped atop Bill.

She sank her teeth into the meaty part of his shoulder. Her new fangs pierced the skin effortlessly and plunged deep into the tissue. She felt an electric tingle run through her facial muscles as she produced thick venom in secret glands, preparing to inject it.

Her husband came awake with a wail and began to struggle, bucking beneath his wife in an effort to dislodge her mouth. The pain was excruciating. He was a strong man, but it was no use. Susan held fast, pinning him to the mattress with superior force. She was so much stronger now. How did she get so strong?

She held him as she focused all her concentration on her new teeth, willing herself to pump the venom in fast and deep. She continued to hold him, still injecting the poison, until he quieted and went still. Only when he could move no more, did she finally stop, sitting up to survey the damage.

Bill lay on his back on the bed, unable to move due to the paralytic effects of Susan's venom. He looked like he was dead, the only thing that betrayed this effect were his eyes, which still tracked Susan's movements, and the soft gurgles that emerged intermittently from his throat. Susan absently stroked one of her new legs, enjoying the smooth feel of the appendage under her hand, as she stared vacantly at his flaccid crotch. The fight had excited her.

She wanted to mate.

Unable to close his drying eyes, Bill looked at the ceiling through a layer of filmy tears as the monster that used to be his wife, employed the tricks she had learned during years of marriage to make his body betray him. He watched in helpless horror while, with patience and practice, she managed to get him erect, a triumphant squeal escaping her misshapen mouth as she mounted him. Rocking her way to release, she coaxed his body into a reluctant climax; a pathetic bubbling sound in his throat was Bill's only acknowledgement of his finish though he longed to cry out.

Her own orgasm followed swiftly, her body pounding his furiously with mindless abandon. Never before had she experienced such sexual pleasure. It washed over her in waves, causing her to cry out her joy, the sound terrifying and alien. Overcome by her own excitement, Susan began to chew furiously.

Moments later, as her sexual high ebbed and Susan regained what little of her senses that remained; she realized that Bill was dead.

She had eaten most of his face.

The wreck that remained no longer resembled her husband at all. With her head tilted curiously to one side, she studied the bloody mess of him. She knew on some level that she should be horrified by what she had done, but she remained calm and emotionless. She poked an inquisitive finger into the empty socket that used to be his eye. It felt warm and squishy in there.

She liked the feeling. She liked the coppery taste in her mouth as well.

Soon her big house would be full again. The sounds of her children scuttling about would ring joyfully throughout the place. Susan glanced at the body that had been Bill one more time. Maybe she would eat the rest later. Right now, she had work to do. She had finally found her *purpose.* After all, the egg sac wouldn't build itself.

As she worked, Susan thought about her daughters. She hadn't seen either girl in a while so she decided to call them both and invite them to come home for a weekend soon. She would schedule it for *after* the eggs hatched. She hoped the girls would be as excited to meet their new siblings as the babies would be to meet them.

ANGEL LUST

"SO, WHAT'S THE CRAZIEST thing you've ever done on screen?" Chantal sipped her coffee, her bright eyes regarding Liza over the mug.

"I let ten guys cum on my face, one after another. Now that was a mess. Oh yeah, and I fucked a Great Dane once." Liza spoke in a loud voice, oblivious to the reactions of the other patrons in the diner. The guy behind the counter shook his head and returned to taking an order, accustomed to the two ex-porn stars and their outrageous conversations. It was after bar rush, when all the college kids fresh from the party and the less desirables mixed together in the diner.

Chantal raised her eyebrows and nodded in appreciation. She'd been getting the wrong kind of attention her whole life, and didn't give a shit what anyone in a diner thought.

Liza signaled for another cup of coffee. Winking at the waiter as he poured it, she waited until he walked away, chuckling at his look of disapproval.

"What about you?" Liza asked.

Taking another sip, Chantal held the cup with both hands and took a moment to ponder before answering.

"Once I had to shake up a beer bottle and shoot it up another girl's ass, then drink it as it poured back out."

"How was that for you?"

"Tasted like shit." Silence for a second, then both women cracked up, their laughter harsh and throaty from too many years of cigarettes and cheap booze. A young couple stood abruptly to leave, twin looks of horror on their faces. The girls returned their stares until the pair was gone, then laughed until thick mascara streaked down their cheeks.

The two had been friends for over twenty years, ever since co-starring together in several adult videos in the early eighties. Liza's short-lived career in the adult entertainment industry had fallen prey to an unfortunate drug habit. Chantal had an overzealous boyfriend with hard fists who beat her burgeoning career into the ground, leaving a twisted mess of scar tissue as a constant reminder. They had both been reduced to prostitution.

Chantal smiled at a young man who stared at her from across the diner, laughing as he quickly averted his eyes from the ruined right side of her face. She leaned across the table, looking both ways to ensure no one was within earshot. Liza looked back at her from across the scarred tabletop, her half-lidded eyes bloodshot and glassy.

"Have you ever heard of angel lust?" Chantal whispered, clearly suspicious of being overheard.

"I've heard of angel *dust*." Liza practically screamed it across the restaurant, causing Chantal to wince and shush her friend.

"Come on, let's go somewhere else." Reaching into her battered purse, Chantal pulled out some change for the coffee and dropped it on the table, then stood to leave.

"Where we going?" Liza asked.

"Somewhere with less ears. Let's go to my apartment. I want to show you something."

Chantal's apartment was actually a room at one of the cheaper motels in town, the kind that rented them by the hour or the week. Liza lived somewhere similar, but a few blocks over. Since the diner was midway between their subsequent turfs, they usually met there for coffee in the early morning hours when they weren't having much luck. Tonight was one such night.

Chantal pressed the key into the lock. A yellow plastic disk embossed with the number 12 bounced against the knob. Pushing open the door, she flipped on a switch, bathing the musty room in muted light. Baby-shit yellow shag carpet, mismatched furniture, and tacky wall-hangings completed the mood. Most surfaces in the room were covered with empty food containers, booze bottles, and condom wrappers. The bed was unmade, its tangled sheets dingy and gray. An unpleasant odor of stale sweat, sex, and booze lingered, but Liza didn't notice it. Her place smelled the same.

"Got any weed?" Liza asked hopefully.

"You know I don't do that shit, Liza. Why you gotta keep asking? There's some vodka in the top drawer."

Liza rummaged through the dresser drawer in search of booze, while Chantal reached under the bed, pulling out a suitcase and retrieving a laptop computer. Pushing a pile of trash off the table top, she set it down and plugged it in. Having found the vodka, Liza wandered over, upended a chair so the garbage fell off and sat it next to Chantal.

"Since when do you have a computer?"

"I've got a regular. He gave it to me." Chantal squinted at the screen as it booted up.

"He pay for the net, too?"

"Nah-I just hacked someone's wireless; one of my johns showed me how."

"So, who's the regular?" Liza tried to keep the jealousy out of her voice.

"Just some guy. Has money. He's into freaky shit and can't get anyone else to do it for him." Chantal negotiated her way through a forum, intent on the screen as she searched for what she was looking for.

"Is he blind?" Liza laughed, but Chantal didn't.

"Yes." If Chantal was offended by Liza's remark, she gave no indication "Here it is! Look at this."

"You know I'm not great with reading; just tell me what it's about." Liza sat in her chair and swigged directly from the bottle, trying hard to focus on her friend.

"Maybe if you weren't so fucking high all the time. Never mind. I'll tell you about it." Chantal turned her chair so she faced Liza but could still see the computer. "There's this guy on the internet. He's always looking for videos and shit. Has some real crazy tastes. Wants videos of bestiality and eating shit and stuff. You know, one of those real sick fuckers. Always wants to watch some chick drinking cum out of a cup or some shit."

Liza nodded knowingly, though she looked bored, picking at her badly polished nails.

"*Anyways,* he's on here. Always a different last name and email address so no one can find him, but you can tell it's him from the messages. So I've seen him around and apparently everyone says he pays good for what he gets, so he's on the level."

Liza rolled her eyes.

"Okay! I'm getting to it. He's on here yesterday and he says he'll pay a million dollars for a video of a chick getting it on with a dude who has angel lust."

"What the hell is angel lust?" The mention of a million dollars instantly cured Liza's boredom. She leaned forward in her chair, all business now.

"I was wondering the same thing, so I looked it up. I guess sometimes when a guy dies, he gets a boner. Like a *permanent* boner. The morticians have ways to make it go away so you're not like staring at uncle Bob in the casket and he's got a big ol' hard-on or nothing, but I guess it happens like that."

"So this dude wants a video of some chick fucking a dead guy? That's some messed up shit, Chantal".

"I know it, but a million bucks? Are you kidding me? I'd fuck anything for a million bucks."

"So why are you telling me about this?" Liza's eyes narrowed in suspicion.

"Cuz I can't do this by myself. Someone has to tape the shit."

"What's in it for me?" Liza still looked uncertain.

"Half."

"Half?"

"Yeah, that's five hundred thousand for each of us." Chantal seemed pleased, but Liza still looked skeptical.

"Would I hafta pay taxes on it?"

Chantal threw up her hands in disgust and stood, grabbing the bottle out of the other woman's hand and taking a big swallow before she began to pace the room, gesturing angrily.

"I don't know why I even bother with you, Liza. Sometimes you're so goddamned dumb I can't stand it. Of course you don't gotta pay taxes on it. Do you pay taxes on your fuck money?"

"Okay, okay. Calm down. I didn't say I wasn't in. I'm just wondering why you would even wanna share it with me. You could always put a camera on the dresser or something." Liza said.

"I know I could. But for a million bucks he's gonna want something good. And besides, you're my only friend—my *best friend*—and I thought this thing might help us both get our lives together. Get us out of these piece of shit motels and away from blowing nasty fucks for food."

"I don't mind blowing nasty fucks so long as they got the money."

"Never mind. I'll do it myself. I thought you might want a better life for yourself. We aren't that young anymore and you can't turn tricks forever."

Liza grabbed the bottle back and took a swig, wiping her mouth with the back of her hand. The cheap vodka burned its way down her throat, warming her belly and making her flush.

"Drop the drama, Chantal. I'm in. So what we gotta do? I don't think we can just walk into the morgue and ask to check out all the dead dude's pricks. It's not Walmart, I doubt they have a *lay-away* program."

"Of course not. We can't exactly get a mortician to let us fuck one of his corpses, either. Well, probably not. The way I see it, we're gonna have to make a case of angel lust."

"Make a case?" Liza was confused again.

"Yeah. I've been looking it up and there's certain ways to die that make it more likely."

"Whoa! Now just wait a minute." Liza held up her hands. "You mean you think we're gonna go around offing dudes in hopes they die with a goddamned hard-on? Are you crazy?"

"It wouldn't be so hard to do. There's plenty of bums around that won't be missed and we can split town as soon as we get the money."

"Yeah, right. And the second the pigs find the body, they come get us cuz we both have records and our prints are on file for hooking."

Chantal shrugged and smiled, "So we wear gloves."

"I don't know. Fuckin a dead guy is bad enough, but I don't know if I can actually *kill* someone, Chantal. That's pretty fuckin heavy."

"I know it is, Liza. It's a big deal, but so is half a million dollars. The cops in this town are too busy to put much time into a dead wino or two, and we can be sitting on some beach a gazillion miles away as soon as we get paid. You know, weed is pretty much legal in Jamaica."

"I don't know. I just don't know." Liza worried at a ragged cuticle. She thought about what it would be like to live in a place where she wouldn't get picked up for drugs. *It would be awful sweet.*

"Well I'm gonna contact the perv. You take a couple days and think on whether you wanna be rich or not."

***

Three days later, Liza and Chantal huddled under an unused bridge sharing a cigarette. A gym bag and a coil of nylon rope sat on the ground between them. It took Liza one whole day to decide she wanted to be rich. Chantal figured the fact she had been roughed up by a john that same night had helped her decide. It was raining out, a fine drizzle that made their bones ache and reminded the hookers they were getting too damn old for this life.

Soon we'll be living on easy street, Chantal thought, discreetly watching a bum stretched out under the bridge. He'd been there for at least forty-five minutes. He seemed to be passed out.

"Okay. What do we do now?" Liza's hands were shaking, more from nerves than the cold. She appeared sober, miserably so. Chantal had insisted she stay as clean as possible for the task. No use making stupid mistakes because she was loaded.

"See that framework on the underside of the bridge? I'll climb up the side and toss the rope through, then you wrap it around his neck. I read that hanging causes the angel lust more than anything else." Chantal held up the noose and Liza looked at it in admiration.

"Where'd you learn to tie a knot like that?"

"My Dad taught me."

"Didn't your old man used to fuck you, too?"

"Yeah. He taught me a lot of things. Now get ready to put it over his head." Chantal started to step away, but Liza gripped her elbow.

"Hold on!" She whispered. "Why do I have to do the noosing? How about I do the climbing."

Chantal rolled her eyes. "Okay, whatever. But you have to be ready to jump down and pull on that sucker with all of your weight if he wakes up. We're only going to get one shot at this."

"Okay, but wait!" Liza grabbed her arm a second time, the vibration from her high-strung body making Chantal feel like her teeth were rattling. "What if someone sees us?"

"Look, Liza. We've been over this a hundred times. Nobody comes around here this late at night. And if someone *was* driving by, they can't see shit that's happening under the bridge from the road, anyway. Now put on your gloves and let's do this."

Liza grabbed her one more time and it took all of Chantal's control not to punch her square in the nose. Though she wouldn't admit it, her own nerves weren't exactly steady, and planning a murder was a whole lot easier than committing one.

"What, Liza?"

"We aren't gonna—I mean, we won't actually fuck him under the bridge, will we?"

"I don't know. I guess we'll figure that out if it works. Now get your skinny ass up there and pass me the rope."

Liza scrambled up the side of the embankment, her feet skidding more than once on the loose dirt and gravel. When she reached the top, she lost her footing and slid back down on her ass, shredding the dish gloves she wore and cutting her palms in the process. When she reached the top again, she grabbed the metal beam. She hoped there was enough glove left to keep her from leaving a palm print, but the metal gave off a shower of rust flakes and she doubted it was smooth enough, anyway. Feeding the rope over the beam, she held on for dear life, not wanting to slide back down before the noose was around the bum's neck.

Chantal grabbed the dangling rope and pulled gently, freeing up enough slack to crawl over to where the guy slept in the dirt. She could smell him before she even got close, and pulled her shirt up over her nose. As she made to slip it over his head, he grumbled and rolled over, muttering gibberish in his sleep before resuming his loud and uneven snoring.

Gently easing the noose over his neck, she started when he farted in his sleep and an involuntary giggle erupted from her mouth. The wino flinched and sat up abruptly, then grabbed her sleeve in his dirty hand.

"What the fuck you doin? You robbin me, bitch?" Chantal pulled back hard, trying to break free of his grip.

"Liza, now!" She scrambled backwards, struggling with the man, who was much stronger than his slender, malnourished body made him appear. He lay on the ground, his filthy hand refusing to relinquish its grip on her shirt.

Liza wrapped the rope around her hand and jumped down, sliding on her ass again and nearly jerking her arm out of its socket when the slack on the rope ended. The noose tightened, and the wino let go of Chantal, his hands flying up to his throat. Wasting no time, Chantal scrambled to her feet and ran to where Liza struggled, gripping the rope in both hands and heaving with all of her might. Both women tugged with all of their weight, lifting the bum until his feet dangled several inches above the ground, kicking and spasming as he made the choking sound over and again.

Chantal lost her grip and fell on her ass, causing Liza to also let go. The man dropped to the ground, still kicking and trying to loosen the rope around his neck.

"Aw shit, grab it!" Chantal jumped to her feet and hauled on the rope again. Liza joined her, and they had him in the air once more. *Why's it taking so long for this heavy bastard to die?* Chantal looked around, desperate to find something that would help gain leverage. She spotted a heavy chunk of broken concrete, an iron reinforcement bar protruding from it.

"Liza. Help me pull this rope over there." She nodded towards the cement chunk. "Maybe we can tie it off."

Liza said nothing, only grunted and nodded, eyes wide with fear and exertion. The two pulled as hard as they could, leaning back on the rope so their combined weight would drag the bum higher into the air.

Like a fish on a line, he swung and arched, fighting for breath and making those horrible gagging noises. They almost dropped him again before finally making it to the hunk of concrete. Chantal wound the rope around the rebar, anchoring her weight to allow Liza to do the tying. Neither spoke, their faces red and sweaty as they strained to finish the chore. When it was tied, they stepped back with uncertainty, ready for the block to shift, but it held.

"Sweet Jesus Jumping Christ!" Chantal wiped her arm across her brow, still huffing for breath.

"I know, right?" Liza staggered over to the block and plopped down on it. With elbows resting on knees, she put her face in her hands and moaned.

Chantal gave her an awkward pat on the back, then walked over to where the wino still hung. He was no longer putting up a fight; his hands had fallen to his sides where he swung gently from the beam. She walked around to face him, taking a quick step back and covering her mouth with her hands when she saw his face. His eyes bulged from mottled, purple flesh, the rope barely visible where it cut into his swollen neck. A stiff tongue protruded obscenely from his mouth. He smelled like shit, but she wasn't sure whether he had crapped himself before or after the hanging. He hung about two feet off the ground, his crotch just below eye level. Chantal shuddered.

"Um, Liza?"

"Yeah?"

"I think he's dead."

"God, I hope so." Liza stood and walked over to Chantal, grimacing in distaste when she saw him.

"So when's this angel lust supposed to happen?" She reached out to touch him, pulling her hand back at the last second.

"I don't know. I guess probably right away." Chantal said.

"Well?"

"Well what?"

"You gonna check or what?" Liza clasped her hands behind her back, clearly not intending to.

"Fuck. Whatever!" Chantal reached out, roughly grabbed the front of his pants, and pulled the zipper down, struggling with the button on the jeans for a moment before it gave. She pulled them down to his knees, taking his boxers with them.

"No hard-on, but it looks like he had a nasty case of *something.*" Chantal wiped her hands on her pants in disgust.

"Do you think it's cuz we dropped him?"

"Christ, I don't know."

"So now what do we do? All that and it doesn't even fucking work. Nice!"

"We try again tomorrow night, I guess. I'll look and see what other deaths cause it. I know it has to be violent."

"Are you shitting me? You want to do this *again?*"

Chantal looked at the dead man swinging from the beam, his blistered penis limp against his furry thigh. If they were lucky, the cops might think it was a suicide, but she wasn't too confident in their luck. She looked Liza in the eye, her own gaze cold and determined.

"Might as well go for it. We're already murderers."

***

Liza knelt before the man in the dirt, trying hard to ignore his body odor. It was hard to do when he kept shoving her head down and mashing her nose into his matted pubic hair. She gagged as her mouth was assaulted by the taste of his bitter sweat, and he laughed.

"Come on now, girlie. I thought you was a pro?" He laughed again, swigging from a bottle of gin, then grabbed her head and gave her face a big, upward thrust. She tried to pull away, but he still held her by the hair. "Not so fast now. You and your little girlfriend made me some promises."

"Yes, we did." Chantal said from behind him, pressing a throw pillow to the back of his head with an ugly- looking revolver jammed against it. The shot was muffled, but it still seemed too loud in the quiet night. The wooded area wasn't too far from the park where they had found him and lured him in with promises of booze and sex.

I hope no one heard that and called the cops, Chantal thought.

Liza shrieked and crab-walked backwards, having been unable to avoid being splattered with blood and brains. The vomit she had tried to hold back erupted out of her mouth and down her blouse in a surprising torrent. She began to sob, tearing handfuls of grass out and scrubbing her face with it. Spying the bottle of gin still clutched in his hand, she pried it out and wiped the neck of the bottle with a clean spot on her shirt, before turning it up and draining it in one gulp. When she was done, she tossed it into the bushes, earning a glare from Chantal.

"Way to leave behind evidence, you idiot. Go get the damned bottle."

Liza scowled back, but did as she was told. She grabbed a flashlight and shuffled off to the bushes. Returning with the empty bottle, she shoved it in her knapsack.

"Did it work?" She looked over at the dead guy, barely able to make him out in the dark. Only one streetlight was close enough to the wooded area to provide any light, but its glow barely penetrated the trees. They could see each other, but little else.

38 | Ad Nauseam

Liza aimed the flashlight, the beam falling on his ruined face before she jerked it away and turned it on his exposed crotch. He had died with an erection, but as they watched, it faded. Along with their hopes.

Liza felt conflicted, upset it hadn't worked, but relieved that one of them wouldn't have to fuck the man. He was nasty enough *before* his face looked like grandma's prize strawberry-rhubarb jam. She also didn't know how they would've dragged his body somewhere remote enough to make their film, while being well-lit enough. The plan had been flawed from the beginning.

Chantal wasn't taking it so well; she swore and sputtered as she kicked the dead man repeatedly in his flaccid cock.

"Stupid . . . fucking . . . idiotic . . . no dick . . . piece of shit! Why can't one of you worthless fucks stay hard?" She finished up by spitting in his ruined face.

"Say, I'm not very smart, but isn't that DNA?" Liza flinched when Chantal turned on her, her face a mask of hatred. The scar tissue twisting down one side was red with rage, and Chantal held her fist back, ready to clobber Liza. She stood that way for several seconds before Liza saw her physically struggling to calm herself. When she was under control again, she spoke.

"DNA won't matter unless we get caught. And we *will* get caught if we don't get this right soon and split town with the money."

"Have you even talked to this guy? How do we know this is real and not some kinda set-up?" Liza felt near hysteria at the thought of getting caught.

"He's for real, alright. I've talked to him."

"When? How?"

"I answered his ad with email and talked to him on the phone."

"The phone? This dude just gave you his number? Sounds like a fuckin cop to me!"

"No, he didn't just *give* me his number. Calm down." Chantal grabbed Liza by the shoulders and pinned her with a level gaze. " I gave him my address in the e-mail, and the next day, some dude in a real nice suit and black car shows up at my door. I tried to ask him questions, but he just hands me this envelope and drives off. At first I thought I was being served for something, but then I realized I ain't got nothing to be sued for. So I open the envelope and there's this cheap cell phone in there, the kind you get at the department stores that you can pay as you go. In the phone was only one number, you know, in the address book. And I call it and it's him. He says call me again when it's a done deal."

"Really? You don't think it's a cop?" Liza looked skeptical.

"No I don't. But there's gonna be plenty of cops looking for us if we don't figure it out. We have to do it now. We get the shot, Dan gets his video, and we get paid so we can split."

"Dan?"

"That's what he said his name was." Chantal waved it off as unimportant.

"So how we gonna do it?"

"Don't worry, I'll figure it out."

Chantal and Liza searched the area for anything they might have left behind that could have fingerprints on it. She gave the orders and Liza obeyed, letting Chantal think she was smarter than she was, and that the other hooker would indeed figure something out.

***

Chantal scowled at the screen, her eyes tired from too much reading. She was getting frustrated at the lack of useful information on the internet. All she could come up with was that angel lust happened to the victims of roughly one in three violent deaths, mostly from hanging, gunshots to the head, or poisoning. Well, they had tried the first two and nothing had happened, but she wasn't sure she could get her hands on any kind of real poison.

Will the third time be the charm? She thought. *What if it's not?* She was starting to lose hope. It had been two days since they offed the guy in the woods and she was fast running out of time to come up with something.

Thunderous pounding on the door interrupted Chantal's musing, and she hurried to it, peaking out of the eyehole. Liza stood on the other side, her head whipping back and forth, looking everywhere at once. Chantal opened the door and Liza rushed in, closing it behind her, as if someone had followed her.

"Get your camera and come with me." Liza said.

"What's going on, Liza?"

"No time. I'll explain on the way. Grab that cell phone from the rich dude, too. Hurry up!"

Chantal grabbed the stuff and shoved it in her purse, then followed Liza out the door. There was a light drizzle falling, and she wished she had grabbed a coat with a hood, but soon forgot her discomfort as Liza explained what happened that evening. By the time they reached the other woman's front door, she felt flushed with excitement, and a little fear. Liza's place looked the same as usual, with the exception of the dead guy sprawled across the bed. He appeared well-kept and clean, his gray hair neatly trimmed.

"Oh my god, Liza! Is it really?"

"Yep." Liza pulled back the sheet thrown across the lower half of the otherwise naked corpse.

"No shit?" Chantal just stared, her stunned face making Liza giggle. "You did it. You fucking did it!"

"Yeah, well, this john rolls up and offers me a hundred bucks for some kink and I bring him back here. So we start getting it on and I start looking at the base of the lamp. I notice how heavy it is and I start thinking about how I could hit him with it. So he's eating my pussy and doesn't even notice that I grab the lamp and I hit him real hard in the back of the head. But it doesn't kill him, just knocks him out, so I wrap the cord around his neck and start pulling. He was already hard when I hit him, but so was that asshole in the park, so I waited half an hour before I came to get you, scared that the boner was gonna go away, but it never did." Liza finished in a rush, her face glowing with happiness.

"You did great! I can't believe it. It sucks that he's in your room, but we'll figure out what to do about that later. Let's get the camera set up and do this. Which one of us is gonna fuck him?"

"Wait now, I killed the dude, so I think it's only fair that you fuck him." Liza stuck her chin out, resolute in her logic.

"Okay, I'll do the fucking, but you need to make sure you get good angles and stuff. We wanna give Dan his money's worth so he doesn't think about stiffin' us."

Liza started giggling and Chantal just stared. "What the fuck's so funny?"

"Stiffin'!" Liza snorted.

"Oh for Christ's sakes! Just get the camera!"

It took them fifteen minutes to get the room set up the way they wanted it, and another ten to adjust the lights to amplify the scene and minimize the shadows cast by the furniture. The john had been dead for well over an hour by the time Liza turned the camera on.

Chantal lubed up his erection, straddled the corpse, and slid onto the dead flesh.

"Do you think I should be using a condom?"

"I don't know, Chantal. It's not like he's gonna cum or anything. What does it feel like?"

"It's really hard but kinda weird. Not cold yet, but not warm either. At least he doesn't smell like a homeless dude."

"Crazy."

"Yeah. Well, let's do this. Remember to only get the good side of my face, okay?"

"Okay. Yeah, I will. Try to act like you like it."

"I'm trying to, it's just really weird. Make sure you get some shots of his cock sliding in and out. Close up, like."

"I am. Real close up. Grab your tits and make a face like you're moaning. We'll edit the sound out. Now lean over and brush them up against his tongue since it's sticking out like that. Go slow and play it up. That's good. That's hot. Do it again."

"What the fuck? Did he just burp? Aw gross! That smells awful!"

"Try not to push on his stomach like that. I think there's some shit squirting out when you do."

"Just get the shots. I don't know how long I can do this."

Chantal performed and Liza taped. For over an hour it went on, until Chantal feared she may throw up from the smell of his stomach gases belching out of his mouth and into her face. She maintained her composure, though, thinking of the million dollars awaiting her.

When she felt they had enough, Chantal told Liza to shut the camera off, enduring one more gust of foul wind as she pressed on his chest to climb off of him. *What the hell did this guy eat?* She didn't see Liza standing behind her until she turned around and bumped into her.

"What the fuck, Liza?" Something cold and hard pressed against her bare midriff.

"I'm sorry, Chantal. But I think I'll be needing the whole million for myself." Liza pushed the blade of the knife in as far as she could, wrenching and twisting when she met resistance. The shocked look on Chantal's face was priceless.

Dumb bitch always thought she was so much smarter than me, thought Liza.

Chantal fell to the floor, her hands slippery with her own blood, trying to pull the knife out of her guts.

The blade had gone upward, puncturing a lung and stopping her from drawing a breath to scream. As she lay dying on the floor, she could see Liza where she sat calmly at the table, waiting.

"Sorry. I guess I don't need a best friend." Liza watched as the life in Chantal's eyes faded, then gathered a few belongings into a bag. She packed the camera and grabbed the phone out of Chantal's purse. "You won't be needing this."

Grabbing a heavy coat off the hook on the back of the door, she walked out into the night, leaving Chantal's body with that of the dead john.

***

Liza paced across the grass, stopping every few seconds to

scan the park around her. Things hadn't gone the way she had hoped when she called Dan. Just thinking about the conversation made her angry.

My deal was with Chantal, not you. I suppose I can work with you, but I'm going to need a little something extra. Dan sounded cold and confident on the phone, and she couldn't exactly argue with the man. *Take it or leave it. It's not like you can take me to court for breach of contract.*

"Where the fuck are you?" Liza spoke in a low voice. The longer she had to wait, the more antsy she became. It felt like she'd been pacing in the park for hours. Finally, a black sedan pulled up to the curb on a side street. The driver's window was darkly tinted, the occupant little more than a shadow in the seat. Moving cautiously, she walked over to the vehicle.

When she was a few feet away, the driver's window slid down several inches without a sound, giving her a partial view of a man's face from the nose up. From what she could see, he was dark haired, but his eyes were hidden behind sunglasses.

"Liza?" The voice was even, emotionless.

"Who wants to know?"

"I'm an associate of Dan's. Get in the car."

"I was supposed to meet Dan here. I'm not dealing with anyone but Dan." Liza raised her chin, her eyes narrowed.

"Dan doesn't do this sort of thing, That's what he pays *me* for. Get in or don't. I'm leaving." The window started to close as silently as it had opened.

"No, wait." Cursing under her breath, Liza walked around the front of the car, opened the passenger door and slid onto the leather seat. Once inside, she turned towards the driver as he pulled away from the curb and smoothly accelerated. He was handsome in a brutal way. His suit looked expensive. The dark glasses kept his expression hidden from her when he glanced over.

"So where are you taking me?"

"It's not far."

"Are you taking me to Dan? I usually don't trust guys like you to just take me places." Liza bit her lip, hating the way she babbled when she was nervous.

"Don't worry. It's not far. You have the video?"

"Yeah, but I'm not giving it to anyone but Dan. What's your name anyways? I don't like riding with some dude and not knowing who he is."

"You can call me Mr. White." For the first time he looked at her and smiled, causing Liza to flinch.

***

"Wake up."

Mr. White's voice cut through the fog in her head, and Liza opened one bleary eye. The other was swollen shut and ached with each beat of her heart. The bright lights caused her to squint and intensified the pounding in her head. A glance around and she realized she was still in the same room. Nylon ropes held her upright in a chair and burned the flesh of her wrists and ribs when she tried to move. She was naked and cold.

"Are you awake?" The sound of his voice caused her to flinch. He hadn't spoken a word to her since they walked into the room. Not even during the beating. "Good."

"What do you want from me?" Liza's voice was hoarse from screaming, her throat burned when she spoke. Blood dripped from her nose, rolling over her split upper lip and into her mouth. She ran her tongue across the inside of her teeth, encountering an open spot. *Fucker knocked out one of my teeth.*

"It's not what I want from you, honey. It's what *Dan* wants. I took a look at that video you girls made and I think it's pretty good. A little editing and it will do just fine." He ruffled her hair affectionately. When Liza tried to pull away from his touch, Mr. White laughed.

"I figured you'd be glad that you didn't do all that work for nothing." Mr. White adjusted one of the two cameras that sat on tripods. They had been pointed at Liza since he'd tied her to the chair, catching every squeal of pain and meaty thud while he beat her for the last many hours.

"Let me go. *Please.* I'll do anything you want."

"Anything? Interesting prospect, but I don't think so."

"I'll blow ya. I'm real good at it."

He threw back his head and laughed, his eyes twinkling. "No offense, honey, but I wouldn't fuck you if *you* paid *me*. If this was about sex, I would've just raped you."

"The money? I'll split it with you."

"Split it with me? Are you kidding?"

"Okay." Liza heard herself whining but was in too much pain to care. "You can have it all. Just let me go."

Mr. White shook his head and retrieved a briefcase from the floor. He set it on a chair and pushed the buttons, turning it so she could see what the case contained. Harsh light reflected off what seemed like a hundred exotic tools, all shiny metal and very *sharp*. He presented them proudly, first to the cameras, then to her.

"It's nothing personal, you know. This'll be easy. All you have to do is act and *react* naturally. Piece of cake. Dan was willing to pay one million for an angel lust video." He picked up a wicked looking meat fork with curved tines, tilting his head as he examined her body, looking for the appropriate place to begin. His smile was gentle but his eyes remained hard as he placed the pointed prongs against Liza's trembling abdomen. The muscles in his forearm bunched as he applied enough pressure to puncture flesh, earning an agonized wail in return. "But he will pay me five million for a *snuff film*."

RETIREMENT WOES

WILLIAM HAD NEVER BEEN a cruel person before the squirrel moved onto his roof.

Two weeks into summer vacation, fourteen long days after he had bid his students farewell for the last time, William sat at the kitchen table in his boxers and white t-shirt under a tattered blue robe. A bowl of oatmeal sat untouched on the table next to the unread newspaper spread out before him.

Staring at the clock on the wall, he watched the minutes tick past and wondered what he was supposed to do with the rest of his life.

"William, will you please mow that lawn today?" His wife, Kristi, walked through the kitchen and into the dining room, a cloud of soft, floral perfume left floating in her wake. Smartly dressed in a peach blazer and skirt with her gray hair perfectly coiffed atop her head in a twist, she was ready for her day as a personal banker, the job she'd held since their kids had all started school.

"Hmmph." William grunted, glancing at his wife, then returning his eyes to the clock.

"Oh William, really. Are you going to mope around here forever? How are you going to handle retirement if you can't even find something to do for the summer? You're *used* to having summers off." Kristi pulled out a chair and perched lightly on the edge, grabbing his hand in her own and frowning. "Have you been taking those pills the doctor gave you?"

"I'm not depressed." William also frowned, but it felt diluted in comparison to his wife's stern countenance. Everything about her personality had always been more forceful, more vibrant. He had no delusions about who ran their household. "I'm just bored."

"You know what you need, William?" Kristi's favorite pastime had always been telling William what he *needed*. "You need a hobby. Rachel's husband builds model cars and Ralph across the street does all that woodworking."

"Those are old man hobbies."

"We aren't getting any younger, dear." She patted his hand affectionately, but he pulled his own back.

"I'm not that old." The whiny tone in his voice made him feel like a petulant child.

"Really, William? So what is this? Sitting around in your shorts all day feeling sorry for yourself? I swear, the least you can do is go out and get rid of that damned squirrel."

"Squirrel?"

"Yeah. The squirrel that's on the roof making Devon bark. Can't you hear him? Or are you going deaf too?" Kristi stood and retrieved her purse, her back stiff and her chin raised in anger. With her hand on the doorknob she turned slightly, her eyes narrowed as she spoke. "You need to do something with yourself, William. I will not spend the next thirty years watching you give up and rot in that chair."

William watched the door slam behind her. Standing to take a shower, he paused when he heard Devon begin to bay in the backyard.

He does sound upset about something, he thought, opting to forego the shower and just get dressed so he could investigate.

On his way to the door, William tripped over something, nearly falling on his face. He heard things go flying, and to his dismay, realized he had knocked over Kristi's massive sewing kit, spilling about a hundred spools of thread.

Even when she's not here she is making my life hell! Why does one woman need that much thread, anyways? Gathering together the spools, Devon's baying continued, now louder and longer.

Devon wagged his tail in greeting and William rubbed the hound dog's graying muzzle.

"Just you and me now, old boy. Two old hounds with nothing to do." William went to the garage and got the dog's food bowl, filling it from a bag on the shelf. There was a time when he just left the bowl out, feeding Devon whenever it ran empty, but the vet said he was getting fat. The weight wasn't good for his heart.

William's doctor had said the same thing about him.

Leaving Devon to his meal, William went back into the garage to get the lawnmower. It was still clean and shiny, a self-propelled model that his three grown children had pitched in for an early Father's Day gift. The old mower had worked just fine, but they worried he was getting too old to push the heavy thing around the yard.

I'm not old, he thought, *never been sick a day in my life. I'm still useful.*

William was halfway through mowing before Devon began to bark again, sitting on his haunches under the eave that jutted above the back porch. Usually the dog was timid around the lawnmower, but he refused to budge when William came near, forcing him to kill the mower. Devon's attention remained on the roof, his bark sounding vicious and the hair standing up on his back.

"What is it, pal? What are you barking at?" William shaded his eyes with one hand and looked up. Devon barked again, and he gently placed his other hand on the dog's head to quiet him. After a moment of mostly silence, filled only with the annoying buzz of cicadas in the trees, he heard it. The high-pitched, distant chittering of a squirrel. A fuzzy red plume of tail appeared, zigzagging across the roof.

"Hey squirrel!" William didn't actually expect the rodent to respond and he laughed in surprise when it peeked over the edge, fixing him with beady black eyes. Devon let loose with a whiny growl as the critter balanced on the gutter, his front half hanging over the edge. The squirrel screeched his indignation as his tiny paws balled up into fists that shook with rage. William nearly doubled over with laughter at the sight.

"Okay little guy. I understand how you feel, but how about you move on so my wife doesn't make me get rid of you?" William felt an unexpected affection for the irate trespasser, an admiration for his bravery and stubbornness when facing a larger opponent. Still, he wasn't about to listen to Kristi bitch about the squirrel all summer. Devon *woofed* in agreement.

Grabbing the industrial pooper scooper he had bought at the farm-and-fleet store last fall, William set about the unpleasant task of cleaning up Devon's mounds of poo. The dog usually sat by the fence and watched with a suitably apologetic look on his old face, but today he didn't bother. Remaining seated, the hound continued to growl low in his throat, his eyes never leaving the roof where the squirrel balanced on the gutter, still shaking his tiny fists and squawking.

Sighing, William shook his head on his way to the garage.

"Okay, little guy. Don't say I didn't warn you."

William pulled the ladder from where it hung, neatly, on wall pegs. He knew there was rodent poison somewhere. After a few minutes of looking and cursing, he found the half-full box of pellets and shook some into his hand. Dropping the poison into his pocket, he picked the ladder up and carried it over to the porch. The squirrel had given up on chastising Devon and was now leaping from the roof to a nearby tree branch and back, high above the dog's head. Taking exception to the obvious taunting, Devon growled at the critter.

"That's enough, squirrel. Quit picking on my dog."

He set the ladder against the house, checking it for stability before climbing slowly up the rungs.

At the top, William reached into his pocket and grabbed the poison, arranging a loose pile of pellets in the gutter. The squirrel hopped over to the tree branch and screeched once, watching as William picked leaves off the roof and shoved the poison into a heap.

Poor little guy. William felt bad about killing the squirrel. He had always found the rodents kind of cute and fun to watch as they hopped across the lawn, their tails twitching and flowing like a gymnast's ribbon. But Kristi wanted him dead, and he made a point to ensure his wife always got what she wanted.

"It's you or me, bud. Come and get it."

The rusty-colored visitor watched from his tree branch as William took down the ladder and put it away.

When William emerged, he saw the empty branch still swaying, the loud- mouthed rodent back on the roof and approaching the pile of pellets suspiciously. Still feeling a bit guilty, he patted the dog on the head and opened the back door.

"Come on, Devon. We can still get a nap in on the couch before Kristi gets home."

***

"William? Please tell me you didn't have that filthy dog in this house." Kristi stood in the doorway, her finger pointing at the living room sofa.

"Hmmm?" William reclined in his EZ Chair, the television remote resting on his outstretched thigh.

"There's dog hair all over the couch. Did you have Devon on the couch? You know how I feel about animals in the house."

"No, dear. Of course not."

"Then how did all that nasty hair get on there?"

"I don't know. Maybe it fell off my clothes."

Kristi crossed her arms and glared at William.

"Did you get rid of that squirrel?"

"Yep. Poisoned him. He should probably be dead by tomorrow." William hated it when Kristi prattled at him during one of his shows. He also hated that she never let Devon come in the house.

That dog's better company than you most days, anyways, he thought, tuning her out. Their marriage had been passionate in the early years, and William figured this was just the way it went with relationships. A comfortable contempt just settles into the vacancy left when love fades.

"Are you even listening to me?" Kristi had her hands on her hips, a posture that never failed to irritate William.

"What?" He flicked the power button reluctantly, stopping Peter Griffin mid-sentence.

"I *said,* make sure you find the corpse so it's not stinking up the yard. The last thing we need is for Devon to eat that diseased little creature and puke it up on the couch when he's *not* in the house."

"Okay. I'll look for it tomorrow morning."

"And take one of your pills," she added, perching on the arm of the recliner to give him a light hug and kiss before going to bed.

"I'm not depressed."

***

"Come on, boy! Get the frisbee." William heaved the plastic disk over Devon's head but the dog merely watched it fly. Yawning, he stretched out in the grass and stared at William expectantly, as if to say, *Cool trick, now go get it.*

"Lazy dog." William laughed and retrieved the Frisbee. He climbed the steps onto the back porch to grab a beer, when something small bounced off his head and rolled across the wood.

"What the hell?" Leaning over to pick it up, he realized it was a pellet of rat poison. Two more pellets hit him and he looked up, just in time for a third to hit his nose. The squirrel was once again perched on the edge of the gutter, pelting him with the poison. The little beast then threw the rest over the edge and screeched at him in indignation.

"Well, I'll be damned. You little bastard." William gathered up the remaining pellets and tossed them in the trash can, mindful of Devon eating it. He was halfway amused, but also a bit angry. "That's it. You've got this coming."

It took a while to find it, but he discovered his son's old pellet gun tucked away in a dusty box in the garage. William grabbed the ladder once again on his way out. This time the squirrel held his ground on the roof, squawking at the intrusion as William climbed the rungs and braced his elbows on the shingles. He hadn't fired a gun of any kind in many years and the first pellet went high and wide.

The rodent fled at the sound of the gun, as the next pellet hit it square in the shoulder. It jumped high into the air, squealing and chittering. Expecting the creature to run away, William was surprised when it turned back to him and charged, its large teeth bared.

Hurrying to retreat, William's foot slipped on the ladder and his chin hit the top rung painfully, causing him to bite his tongue in the process. He scrambled down the ladder and out into the middle of the yard, where Devon waited, yapping.

"That's right, Devon. You tell him, boy." William wiped his chin and his hand came away wet with blood. Glancing up at the roof, he couldn't see the squirrel anymore.

Good. Maybe the little bastard will stay gone now.

***

"What happened to your face?" Kristi moved his hands away as he tried to prevent her from tracing the bandage on his chin.

"I slipped on the ladder and hit my chin. It's not a big deal."

"Why in God's name were you on the ladder?"

"I was shooting that squirrel. The lil' bugger wouldn't eat the poison, so I shot him with Max's pellet gun." William tried grinning, but it made his chin sting.

"Maybe we should take you in to see the doctor." Kristi gave him a look of concern.

"I told you I'm fine." He hated that concerned look more than anything. Even when she was harping on him, something he was used to after decades of marriage, she always had that half-worried look on her face. She acted like he was crazy sometimes, or a child that needed to be reminded of the most basic tasks. William had buried his own mother five years ago, and didn't need a substitute.

"Did you take your pill?"

"Goddamnit, Kristi! I am not depressed. There's nothing wrong with me. I got hurt trying to get rid of a squirrel. That's all. The same damned squirrel you've been riding my ass to kill." William was surprised at the venom in his response. He hadn't known he was angry until he started yelling.

Kristi stared at him, blinking back tears. Unable to deal with his wife at the moment, he turned and stalked out of the room, hearing the first of her sobs as he walked away.

***

The next morning, William awoke to Devon's barking outside and the phone ringing on the nightstand. He turned to discover Kristi's side of the bed was empty.

Must still be miffed from last night. Throwing his legs over the edge of the bed, he sat up and reached for the telephone on the nightstand.

"Hello?"

"Oh thank God, Dad! It took you so long to answer, I was just about to hang up and call the cops."

"What are you talking about, Max?"

"I've called you three times this morning, Dad."

"You have? I guess I was just sleeping soundly. What's the big emergency? I mean, it's not like I'm not happy to hear from you son, but what's going on?" William hadn't talked to his son in close to a month, but he knew that his oldest was busy with his job and family. He missed his kids and grandchildren though, and was disappointed to hear from Kristi that they weren't going to be able to get together over the summer.

"We need to talk. You might want to sit down."

William's pulse picked up as a rush of adrenaline spurred his heart on, though he kept his voice level. "I am sitting. What is it?"

"I hate to be the one to do this, but if I don't, I don't think anyone else ever will. I never agreed with the way Mom chose to handle this, but I'm tired of her calling me at night crying. You need to be told."

"Whoa. Slow down, Max." William felt a throb develop in his

right temple and was unable to follow where his son's conversation was going. "What are you talking about and what is this about your Mom?"

"She's worried sick about you, Dad." Max paused. "We all are. You've been acting strange and you won't take your medication like the doctor says —"

"Now hold on a damned second. I don't know what your Mom has been telling you, but I'm fine. I don't need any pills. I'm not depressed." William felt himself getting angry. Kristi had no business calling and getting the kids all riled up over nothing.

"Those pills aren't for depression, Dad. They're for dementia."

The sun still shone brightly in his eyes, and Devon was still barking his ass off outside, but William didn't notice any of it. His mind froze, trying to grasp Max's words.

"What?"

"You heard me, Dad. You're losing it. And Mom doesn't know how much longer she can deal with this by herself."

"I don't know what the fu-, what the hell you are talking about." William paused and rubbed his temple, fighting a losing battle against his temper. "But there is *nothing* wrong with my mind."

"Really? What do you remember from yesterday, Dad?"

"I did some yard work, and I had a fight with your Mom." William snapped, suddenly very tired and wanting to slam the phone down to silence the accusations.

"That's all? That's really all you did? What did you have for lunch? For supper?"

"I don —"

"That's right. You don't know. You've been losing time for months now. It was Mom's idea to tell you that the pills were for depression, but I always thought you should be told. Especially after losing your job like that."

"I retired."

"Oh, for Christ's sake, Dad! You didn't retire. You were *forced* to resign. You can't tell me you've completely forgotten or suppressed or whatever what you did. You whipped your dick out in the middle of class and pissed in the trashcan. You're just lucky that no one pressed charges for indecent exposure."

William dropped to his knees, unaware he had even stood up. His skin felt cold but he was hot inside, his guts churning. He felt like his whole world had just been turned upside down.

Flashes of half memories began to assault him, but blessedly flitted away again. Emotions rolled within him; anger, shame, and confusion battled against one another until his head felt like someone was hammering it.

Something rolled across the roof and Devon howled, snapping William out of his torment. The phone was still in his hand, the sound of his son's voice far away. Not listening to what Max said, he put the phone to his ear and spoke in an even voice that sounded alien to him.

"I love you, Max, but shut up. I have to go." He put the phone back on the cradle and rose to his feet, his legs numb and shaky. There was a scrambling sound from the roof and he looked up, as if he could somehow see through the upper floors and the rafters to the shingles above.

The squirrel.

William stumbled into the master bathroom and retrieved a can of *Aquanet* hairspray from the counter. He shook it and sprayed a fine mist, checking to make sure the nozzle wasn't clogged. The smell made him smile, for a second he remembered making out with Kristi long ago in his Buick, the lovely scent of her perfume and sweat mingling with her hairspray.

In the junk drawer he found a lighter and flicked it, getting a long flame on the second try. They had both quit smoking when the grandkids were born, but Kristi loved candles and always had a lighter around. Not giving any thought to the fact he still wore nothing but his ratty bathrobe over his boxers and customary white t-shirt, William walked outside.

The ladder was still up against the side of the house and he paused, scratching his head. He thought he had put it away. He never left his stuff out. Something wet bumped his hand and he actually screamed, pulling it back in. Devon let out a concerned *woof* and cowered, fearful of being struck. The sight made William's heart ache.

"Oh Jesus, boy. You really scared me." He scratched the dog behind an ear and Devon kicked one back leg in response, blissfully trying to scratch an imaginary itch. William stared up at the roof, seeing only the occasional fluff of the squirrel's tail as it strutted around.

His mind spun with bits of his conversation with Max as well as images of things he had forgotten he'd done, like screaming at his class, a fight with Kristi. Had he hit her? *Could I ever hit her?* He shut the thoughts out, his focus on nothing more than that taunting red tail and the smug little rodent it was attached to. His anxiety and fear formed into a ball of white-hot rage, causing bile and acid to churn and eat at his stomach lining.

"You little son of a bitch, I'm getting you once and for all." William gripped the can of hairspray in one hand and climbed the ladder using his free one. When he reached the top, he swung one butt cheek onto the roof, his free hand grabbing the shingles for support. He felt cold inside, an icy resolution stealing his nerves. "Come on, you bastard. This ends today."

The squirrel held his ground, locked in a stare-down with William that lasted several moments. Neither made a sound as William reached into his pocket to retrieve the lighter. He waited, but the squirrel simply stared, not coming close enough for him to get it. He could see a wound on its shoulder where he had shot it with the pellet gun, but it had scabbed over and the squirrel didn't appear any the worse for wear.

Devon let out a howl, startling William, and he almost slid off the roof. He glanced at the dog and heard an awful screeching, turning in time to see his tormentor come barreling across the shingles towards him. He didn't have time to aim, simply pressed the button on the aerosol can and flicked the lighter.

The flame was impressive, shooting out several feet and igniting the rodent. He realized too late what was going to happen and leaned backwards to avoid the squealing, flaming demon that hurtled towards him like a bullet. Losing his footing and pinwheeling his arms, he fell from the roof. Then his head hit the ground and the world went black.

***

William really wanted to stay asleep, but something warm and wet kept smacking him in the face. A high-pitched whining intruded on his slumber and the wet thing moved to the side of his head. This caused a flash of pain that made his eyes pop open, only to close back to slits as the afternoon sunlight stabbed his brain. Then Devon's jowly face mercifully blocked out the sun, and a renewed round of licking ensued.

"Devon. Stop." William chuckled weakly and tried to push the dog away. *Why am I on the ground? Did I faint? Was it a stroke?* He was confused, and when he tried to sit up, a thunderous pain ripped through his skull. Then he remembered.

The squirrel.

He slowly did a careful inventory of injuries. His head still thumped and his ribs on the right side were a mass of radiating agony, but other than that he felt fine. Sitting up slowly, he saw a decent- sized rock covered in blood where he'd been laying.

Must've hit my head on the bastard. Lucky I didn't split my fool skull open. Probing the wound on the side of his skull with shaking fingers, he decided his original assessment may have been premature. His head didn't feel exactly *intact* anymore.

That left the mystery of his ribs, but he quickly surmised what had happened when he saw a ceramic lawn ornament shattered on the grass. He'd landed on the thing, pieces of white glass protruded from the side of his chest, and he marveled at how little alarm he really felt, considering he didn't know how deep they went or if he had punctured a lung. Something moving on his right caught his attention and he gaped at what lay next to him on the lawn.

"You tough little shit!" William said with wonder and more than a small measure of respect as he watched the squirrel struggle to get upright. The thing was nearly hairless, its skin scorched and blistered. Apparently blinded by the fire, his beady black eyes were now a milky color. Alternating between squawks and mewls, it still appeared as though it were trying to come at him. Dragging limp back legs and a charred tail, it slowly and what had to have been painfully made its way across the grass, teeth bared. Devon backed up and growled.

"It's okay, boy." William said, grabbing the bloody rock that had left a dent in his skull. It was heavy and sharp in his hand as he lifted it over his head to smash the squirrel, but he froze in position. His head thumped and swam, his thoughts a jumble of confusion surrounded by a red mist of agony. He couldn't do it. He knew it would even be a kindness at this point, to put the creature out of its obvious misery, but he found himself admiring its spirit. Crippled and dying it still came, dedicated to its cause.

William dropped the rock as bitter tears ran down his face. He thought about how he must appear from the outside. Thought about what he was on the inside.

I'm useless and old. And I'm losing my mind. I can't even vanquish a squirrel. I'm just an old man with an old dog, weeping in my yard. William wished more than anything that he had died in the fall. He was an embarrassment to his family. A burden on his children and wife.

Guilt gave way to anger in a flash. It was Kristi who had caused all of this, Kristi who forced him to hurt the squirrel.

It's her constant nagging that's driven me crazy. The stress of putting up with her harping all those years had caused a nervous breakdown of some sort. I'm not demented, just plain fed-up! She has even turned my son against me. William thought about the way Max had spoken to him. His harsh, accusatory tone. He thought about his job. Never gone a single day due to illness, and they pushed him out the second something started to go wrong with his mind. But not Kristi, her mind was *just fine.*

Something tugged at the hem of his robe and he looked down, watching as the squirrel bit the terry cloth.

The stubborn little bastard made it. He felt an overwhelming sympathy for the beast roll through his chest, constricting his lungs so he couldn't draw a breath. The anger flared anew, almost crippling in its intensity. In that moment he knew what he should do. His head was fuzzy again and he was having trouble keeping his thoughts straight as memories and emotions warred with darker images he didn't want to see. He knew what he could do to make it all better for him and the squirrel.

Rising to a painful crouch, William cupped his hands around the squirrel, wincing only slightly when the rodent sunk its large, yellow teeth into the pad of flesh at the base of the thumb. He cradled it to his body and slowly climbed the porch steps, each step making his head and ribs sing out a duet of agony. At the back door he stopped and turned towards Devon.

"You coming, old dog?"

The hound looked at his owner, then at the half-dead creature still cradled in his hands. He whined and sat down.

"Suit yourself. I'm going in."

Devon whined again in indecision, then bolted up the steps and slunk through the door before it closed.

***

"Oh Damnit, William." Kristi walked across the lawn to where the ladder still leaned against the back of the house for the second day in a row. "I guess I will have to put it away myself. And what's this?"

The shattered remains of her favorite lawn ornament lay in the grass and she felt her irritation ramp up another notch, until she noticed the pool of sticky blood. A crimson- smeared rock lay close by, as well.

Oh no! William.

She had feared this day would come. For months Kristi had left for work every morning wondering if it was safe to leave William alone. She had fought with her oldest son for months about whether they should tell him what was going on, but William had *some* pride and she couldn't bring herself to hurt him. Now she may be too late.

Her high heels caught on the steps and she fell forward in her haste to get into the house, tearing her panty hose and skinning one knee. Climbing back to her feet, she flung open the door, calling out to her husband in a panic-stricken voice.

"William!" The lights were off and all the blinds closed, casting the interior of the kitchen in gloomy shadow. Kristi smelled the dogshit a second before she stepped in it and slid, her hand grabbing the counter to keep from falling.

"Ouch!" Something jabbed her palm. A sewing needle had pierced the flesh of her palm and she could see her sewing kit open on the counter. A small cry escaped her as she pulled it out with her teeth. The cry was echoed by a whine from across the room.

"Devon?"

The dog whined again but didn't approach. Kristi reached for the light switch, freezing when William's voice broke the silence.

"Don't. The light hurts his eyes." His voice sounded strange, groggy.

"William? Are you okay? What's wrong with Devon?" She reached for the switch again.

"I said *don't!*"

Kristi recoiled as if struck. She could see William's silhouette in the doorway but little else. Something cold and wet touched her hand and she screamed, realizing belatedly that it was just Devon. He sat in front of her, whining and growling low in his throat, though William ignored him.

"I always wondered why you had so many spools of goddamned thread in your sewing kit. Who the hell *needs* all that thread?"

Kristi flicked the light switch, bathing the kitchen in a glow from the chandelier. She winced when she saw her husband, his hair matted with gore and the side of his blue robe dark with blood.

"Oh William. What happened to you?" She took one step toward him, then stopped when his lip turned up in a sneer, his eyes wild and darting.

"You wanted that goddamned squirrel gone."

"William, you're hurt. Let me call someone. Your head wound looks *really* bad."

"Great idea. Why don't you call that doctor that you're

probably fucking. Or better yet, call my son so you two can talk about how *crazy* I am."

As he took slow steps towards her, his robe fell open and Kristi saw something on his side *wiggle*. Her mouth opened for a scream that wouldn't come when she saw the atrocity sticking out from his side. Mangled and burned, its eyes scorched blind and milky, a squirrel jutted from his ribs. The thing squealed at her and she felt her bladder let loose, warm urine running down her legs. Thick, dark stitches held the creature to William's skin, haphazard sutures still weeping blood. The thing struggled to be free, its teeth clicking shut as it cried out, straining the thread and tearing its own flesh in the process.

"Oh Jesus, William! What have you done?"

"Oh dear. Did you just piss yourself? Who's old now? It's okay, Kristi." He took another step towards her and she realized he held something dark and sharp in his other hand. The poker from the fireplace. "I almost killed him because of you. You animal-hating bitch. But's it's okay. I fixed him. My body is still strong. It will heal him."

William raised the poker over his head, his eyes bright with insanity as the dog growled and his wife shrieked.

"Shhhhhh, it's okay, babe. I know there's something wrong with my head. But it's going to be all right. I mean, you have enough brains for both of us. And we have plenty of thread . . . "

MICAH'S MUSE

$\mathbf{M}$ICAH HAD ALL BUT given up on his dream of becoming a writer on the day that he met Muse. When he graduated from school with his Bachelor's Degree in Creative Writing, he'd been filled with fantasies of becoming a best-selling horror author. Despite his professor's constant harping that he should not write genre fiction, he still loved horror and planned to make his writing career with scary novels. He knew he'd have to start somewhere else first, so he took a position at the newspaper as a copy editor, telling himself it was just until he landed his first contract with a major publisher. Five years later, long years filled with writer's block, interrupted by inconsistent streaks of stories that led to stacks of rejection letters so tall they fell to the floor every time he sat at his desk, Micah still worked at the paper, editing articles written by other people.

Micah learned all of the skills he needed to be a professional writer; but with perfect grammar, stellar clarity, and top notch mechanical skills, he still lacked the one thing he needed most: a story to tell.

No matter what he tried, he couldn't seem to come up with a tale worth telling. Even his most exciting ideas fizzled out as soon as he moved from planning and note-taking to writing. The few projects he'd finished came back rejected every time he submitted to a new market. The rejections, generic form letters that did nothing to help him hone his craft, usually just said his story wasn't a *good fit* for them. Even his mother quit supporting his dream a couple years ago. She changed the subject whenever he brought it up now, no longer offering words of encouragement.

With his head full of thoughts of giving up and resigning himself to the life of a newspaper editor, Micah didn't notice the old woman until she spoke his name.

"*Micah.*"

Halting mid-step, he looked around, startled out of his reverie by the eerie voice. The sun shone brightly that day, but he felt cold as he glanced down at the woman squatting on the sidewalk in front of his apartment. A dense clump of trees at the building's corner obscured most of her in shadow.

"Do I know you?"

"No, but I know all about you, Micah."

The woman leaned forward from her crouch and became visible in the bright sunlight. Micah almost recoiled at the sight of her. As if she could sense his discomfort, the crone smiled, her few remaining teeth black with rot and her hair a snarled nest of greasy gray. Her clothing was filthy and repaired so many times that it seemed there was more *patch* to the dress than original material. On her feet was a pair of scuffed men's loafers.

"Who are you?" Micah tried to look beyond the grime in an attempt to recognize her, but he felt certain he had never seen the old gal in his life. *I'd remember someone this hideous.*

"How about you just call me Muse."

"Muse?"

"Yeah. That'll do."

Dark eyes of indeterminate color glittered from within the folds of a face so deeply lined and dirty that Micah thought a month of baths wouldn't get it clean. The intensity of her gaze coupled with her repulsive smile made him uneasy. *She doesn't look like much of a threat, but street people can be crazy and unpredictable,* he thought.

Time to move along. He started to step away.

"Now hold up, Micah." Muse rose to her feet, moving more gracefully than he would've expected, though her joints popped as she stood. She hovered in the shadow cast by Micah's towering frame. "I've got something for you, boy. Something you need mighty bad right now."

Rummaging in a bag hanging over one hunched shoulder, she eventually pulled out a piece of paper to give him. When he didn't take it, she thrust it at his hand, impatience darkening her creased face.

"Take it!" she snapped, and he reluctantly took the note and read it, barely able to discern what the spiky writing said. It looked like a website.

"What's this?"

"What does it look like? Go type that in on the fancy computer you got in your office, and it'll show you a contest for an anthology that's taking submissions right now."

"So what am I supposed to do about that?" Micah thought this whole episode with the strange woman seemed surreal.

"You're gonna submit a story, stupid! And you're gonna *win*." Muse grinned again and let out a cackle.

"Listen lady. No disrespect, and I don't know where you're getting your information about me, but I'm not a writer. I don't have anything to submit." Micah tried to hand the paper back, but she held up one claw-like hand in refusal. He noticed her fingernails, long and twisted things, thickened and rimmed with black grime.

"Sure you do! You just don't know it yet." The blackened nubs of Muse's teeth protruded haphazardly from diseased gums. Her horrible laughter turned into a wretched cough that folded her in half and made Micah fear she'd choke. He instinctively reached a steadying hand toward her, grimacing at the liquid hacking noises she made.

Without hesitation, Muse's hands shot out with unnatural speed and clamped on either side of Micah's face, fingers hooking behind his ears. He didn't have time to react as she spoke a few words in a language he didn't recognize and pressed hard with her thumbs into the center of his forehead before shoving him away and spitting an enormous wad of green phlegm at his feet.

"*You crazy bitch!*" Micah nearly fell on his ass as he stumbled back from the crone, rubbing his forehead. He could still feel the heat of her disgusting hands on his face. All traces of mirth left her face and when she spoke her voice carried a hint of menace, making goose bumps stand up along his arms despite the heat of the afternoon.

"The first one is free, *Micah.* Now go write your story."

Micah hurried away, looking back only once to see that she had blended back into the shadows once again. It wasn't until he made it up the three flights of stairs and locked the door of his apartment behind him, that he realized he still had the paper clenched in his fist. Shuddering at the memory of her touch, he tossed the scrap of paper into the garbage and went directly to the bathroom, taking a long, hot shower.

Nasty bitch probably gave me herpes! Not bothering to dress after his shower, Micah crawled into bed for a nap. The encounter had left him exhausted and he soon succumbed to a fitful slumber.

***

Micah woke that night disoriented and confused. He'd intended to only sleep for an hour, but the clock on the night table said it was past midnight and the harsh glow of the streetlights flooded the room through the open blinds.

Oh, shit! He had a project due in the morning and had intended to finish it after dinner. Micah crawled out of bed and pulled on a pair of clean boxers before padding barefoot into the kitchen to start a pot of coffee. It looked like he was going to have to pull an all-nighter if he held any hope of meeting the deadline. While the coffee brewed, he walked into his office (originally a second bedroom, but he put a desk and some filing cabinets in there) to turn on his computer.

After retrieving a cup of coffee, Micah returned to his desk with the intention of opening his files and working on the edit that was due in a few short hours, but found himself opening a new document instead. After a few moments of staring at the blank screen, he began to type.

Starting out slow, but gradually increasing in speed, his fingers flew across the keyboard as if on autopilot; and as the story took shape, it seemed to flow straight from his hands rather than his mind. A feeling of excitement like he had never known gripped him as the tale unfolded. Each new word he typed was as completely foreign to him as if he were reading them in someone else's story for the first time.

He sat forward, intently reading to see how the story would end. After typing the last word, he wept, secure in the knowledge that the story wasn't just good, but *great.* Now he just had to submit it, but what did he do with the paper?

Panic bloomed in his gut and he raced into the kitchen, digging through the garbage frantically, trying to find the slip of paper that he wadded up hours before. It sat at the very bottom of the can, as if the importance of it had added actual weight. Micah took the note into the office and typed in the website, gasping at what came up on the screen. It wasn't just *any* publisher and it wasn't just *any* anthology. He immediately recognized the name as being one of the biggest horror publishers in the industry.

My story in this book would be my ticket to the fast lane! After checking the guidelines for formatting preferences, he held his breath and clicked submit.

***

Micah spent the next few weeks writing in an attempt to take his mind off waiting for a response to his submission, but it didn't help much. He knew that most places required at least thirty days and sometimes up to six months before they responded, but still felt himself slipping into a dark depression. He tried to tell himself it was waiting that was doing it, but knew it was the writing that caused his despair. No matter what he did to try and replicate the experience of that night, he just couldn't do it. He had some ideas during that time, even some decent ones, but as before, they turned cold as soon as he tried to put them on paper. He was close to giving up again, when he finally got an email from the editor of the anthology.

Nothing could have prepared him for what it would say.

Not only did they like his story, they *loved* it! The email went on to say that it was the best story they had received in years and they would love to see more of his work. Maybe he had a novel length piece they could review? Micah's heart nearly stopped when reading the editor's opinion that he could be *the fresh voice in horror they had been seeking for a long time.* This response was an answer to his most deeply held prayers. He couldn't believe his luck.

Micah wrote back promising the editor he would provide the synopsis for a full length novel within the next few weeks.

Then anxiety began to set in. He doubled his efforts to come up with something decent, spending all of his free time and even some afternoons at work trying to come up with an idea that would knock them out. As always, it was fruitless. All of his ideas hit a brick wall almost as soon as they popped into his head. Micah felt the pressure to come up with something great destroying him. The only thing worse than never making it at all, was the thought of making it once and never being able to do it again. He would rather die than become a one hit wonder.

He found himself checking the shadows by his apartment whenever he left, hoping to catch a glimpse of a nasty old woman in men's loafers, but she never showed. Then, one afternoon, once his three weeks had almost lapsed and he had given up hope, Muse appeared at the deli.

She looked the same as that day on the sidewalk, maybe a little dirtier, when she sat down in the empty seat across from Micah. Being a creature of habit, he ate lunch at the same deli almost every day and was well known by the workers. The manager raised his eyebrows at Micah from behind the counter before shooting a pointed glance at the old woman. Shaking his head and winking at the man, Micah focused his attention on the hag, who smiled at him with a grotesque gleefulness.

"So you won, eh?" She reached across the table and took what was left of Micah's sandwich, taking a noisy bite of the ham and cheese.

"Yes," he said, glancing at the sandwich in her filthy hand and losing his appetite. "He wants a novel from me."

Muse nodded her head and chewed, not responding. Micah waited, but still she said nothing, obviously enjoying *his* lunch. Micah looked at her, feeling disgusted and more than a little afraid.

"Well?" he asked, tired of waiting for her to respond. "Can you do it again?"

"Uh huh." Muse caught his eyes with a level stare, popping the remainder of the sandwich in her mouth and swallowing before she continued. "But this time it's gonna cost you."

Micah had suspected as much, considering her parting words to him the last time they met.

"How much?" he asked, his tone business-like, as if they were discussing a housekeeping job rather than magic. The whole thing was crazy, but he knew that in some insane way, *she* had caused him to write the last story.

Muse waved her hand dismissively in his face. "I don't want your money."

"What *do* you want?"

"Call your boss and take the rest of the afternoon off. We're gonna take a little walk to your apartment and I'll show ya." With that she stood and walked out the door, not waiting for his response. Micah had already paid for his lunch, so he hurried to catch up, pulling out his cell phone and placing a call to his the office to tell his boss that he had come down with a stomach virus and wouldn't be in for the rest of the day. His apartment was only a few blocks away from the deli and Muse walked much faster than he would've believed she could.

Am I really doing this? Do I really want to let this creepy bitch into my apartment? Muse strutted up the stairs like a woman half her age, then waited expectantly in front of his door.

Who or what the hell is this woman? What if she wants sex?

Micah couldn't imagine how he would ever be able to fulfill his end of the bargain if that was the case.

"How do you know so much about me?" Micah asked, feeling very uneasy about letting her into his home.

"You don't wanna know, boy. Now unlock that door and let me in. We have work to do and I don't have all day to screw around on this."

Micah did as he was told, unlocking the door and entering in front of Muse.

She didn't seem to have much in the way of manners, so he saw no reason that he should go out of his way to act chivalrous to the hag.

Once inside, she spent a few moments peering around, her glittering dark eyes taking in everything in at once. Apparently satisfied with what she saw, Muse pushed a pile of papers off the kitchen table and sat down on the chair.

Muttering incoherently, she wasted no time upending her bag and scattering the contents onto the table. What looked like a pile of stones rested in a heap on top. Irregularly shaped and a mixture of odd colors, the stones, Micah imagined, were probably not rocks at all but rather the faded, glossy bones of small animals.

"Are you a witch?" Micah's voice ended in a squeak, causing color to flood his face.

"Does it matter?" Muse looked up from arranging the bones and stones, her eyes narrowed and her mouth pinched.

"I was just wondering how you, uh, did what you did to me."

"I can explain it to ya, or I can do it again. Which you want?"

"I need a novel. They are expecting a novel out of me and I can't come up with one. I was hoping—"

"I *know* what you need. Now can we get to it?" She looked impatient and he suddenly feared she might leave.

"Yes, of course."

Muse made a show of studying the pattern of the bits and pieces on the table, scrutinizing their layout for long moments before making minor adjustments. When she was satisfied, she nodded her head once and made a horrible phlegmy noise in the back of her throat before hacking a wad of snot a high school bully would've been proud of onto the pile. Micah grimaced.

"Time for your contribution."

"My *contribution?*"

"I told you this one wasn't free. Now get out your pecker, boy. Gonna need some of your spunk for it to work."

"My *what?*" Micah stared at the hideous creature seated at his kitchen table, hoping he had heard her wrong.

"Come on! You jerk off every morning thinking about that reporter with the big tits. So just do it already!"

He stood frozen in place, his jaw slack. *How in the hell could she know that?* Muse made an impatient gesture at his crotch and Micah took a step back.

"I'm sorry. I think this was a mistake."

"I guess so. Maybe you don't wanna be a real writer after all." She stood and made as if to gather her trinkets back into the bag, but Micah grabbed her wrist. She glanced sharply at him .

"I do want to be a writer. I *do.*" Unbuckling his belt and wondering if he had lost his mind, Micah pushed the flaps of his jeans aside and pulled his penis out of the slit in front of his boxers. He rubbed at himself mechanically, picturing the busty reporter while trying not to notice that the old woman's eyes watched his every move with rapt attention. It was no good. He couldn't masturbate with her watching.

"Oh for cripes sake!" Muse spit on her hand and grabbed his flaccid cock before he could pull away, stroking him in a rough and professional manner which left no doubt that she had done this before. To his amazement, he became hard almost immediately. As her gnarled hand gripped him in a fist and worked him relentlessly, he felt himself racing towards a ball-draining climax.

Hideous or not, she was about to get him off in a big way.

"Oh my God!" he shouted, gripping the table with both hands as he came, spurting his *spunk* upon the pile of rocks and bones in what seemed like an endless flow. Hearing a sizzling noise, he looked on in amazement as thin, blue smoke began to rise from the mess.

"God ain't got nothing to do with this. Now breathe it in, boy! Quick, before it stops!"

Micah did as he was told, his head swimming as the sweet smoke filled his lungs. Still clutching at the table, he tried to stop the floor from racing up to meet him, but the world went black as he fell.

Waking a few hours later, Micah lay sprawled on the kitchen floor, his head aching and his cock still hanging limply out the front of his shorts. He sat up, rubbing an egg-shaped lump on the back of his head. The pile of stones on the table was gone. So was Muse.

The memory of that clawed hand jerking him off filled Micah with humiliation and he wanted to vomit, hot bile forcing its way up his throat. He walked with uncertainty towards the bathroom, intending to take a hot shower to wash away the memory, but found himself turning left into the office instead. Through no conscious effort of his own, he turned on the computer and opened a new document. Head still throbbing and stomach churning, Micah began to type.

***

"I'm getting the cue that we only have time for one more question. You, in the back. Yellow shirt."

A shapely blonde in a tight yellow sweater stood up, smoothing her slacks over her hips nervously before speaking.

"Um, yeah. I was wondering. Your books are so great and scary. Where do you get your ideas?" She immediately sat back down, leaning forward in her seat as if she expected him to divulge the meaning of life.

Micah smiled at the woman before sweeping the entire audience with a mock serious look. This was a common question at public engagements, but it was one he enjoyed closing the night with. After a moment of silent contemplation to build the tension, (the blonde looked like she might actually fall off her chair) he spoke.

"My muse is one seriously twisted bitch, and she drives me relentlessly." The MC thanked him and Micah nodded to the crowd before he left the stage to thunderous applause. No matter how many times he did one of these things, he still enjoyed the attention. He knew plenty of bestselling authors who hated these engagements, who resented having to make appearances for the sake of marketing and building a fan base, but not him. He loved the attention and adoration of his fans. He never became annoyed when interrupted during dinner by a fan requesting an autograph. He *deserved* the attention. He went through hell to get where he was now.

As the plane began to taxi down the runway, Micah noticed the woman across the aisle from him reading his latest book, *The Devil's Way*. She smiled shyly at him when she caught him looking and he smiled back, giving her a little wink. Some days he felt like a fuckin rock star. But as the plane got closer to home, his jubilant mood began to sour. His thoughts strayed from the crowd earlier in the night to Muse. The circuit was almost over and a movie based on the book was due to hit the theaters in just two weeks. His publisher would be expecting an outline for his next project very soon.

Muse.

Glancing across the aisle toward the woman once more, he looked at the demonic man on the cover of the book; something about the eyes was familiar. They reminded him of Muse's demented stare. Suddenly he wasn't so happy to see her reading it. He wondered if she would still want to buy his books if she knew the things he did to write them. Then again, with the way the world was, it might increase their appeal.

It had been the same thing after the second book as it had been with the first. Muse disappeared and Micah foolishly told himself he wouldn't need her help next time. He told himself he would finally figure out the formula that would allow him to churn out a bestseller on his own. Then after weeks of agonizing at the keyboard just to type a few words, she showed up. It seemed as though she could smell his *desperation.*

The second book had required he take a life. It had been hard to kill the neighbor's kitten and place its still warm body upon the stones. He liked cats and had nothing against his neighbors, but he *needed* a sequel to the first book. It was on the bestseller list for a solid twenty weeks. The publisher practically got on his knees and begged for another book.

In the long run, Micah figured, one kitten's life wasn't that much to give for fame and fortune, was it? But seeing that broken hearted little girl searching every afternoon after school for her lost pet had really made him feel like shit. Those teary blue eyes had ultimately made him move away. He had made enough money off the first book to buy a house in the country and the sequel was so highly anticipated it was predicted to top the charts upon release. He could certainly afford to move somewhere better, and thought maybe with a change of scenery he would find the formula to write the next novel by himself.

Six months in the country and Micah realized he still didn't have what he needed to write alone. An overwhelming sense of panic sent him back to his old neighborhood where he spent the whole evening roaming, looking for his lost Muse. He searched street corners and diners, even went through the homeless shelter *twice* in his desperate search. Only when the snow became so heavy he feared he might not make it home did he finally give up.

I've fucked up; she can't find me. I can't find her. My career is over.

When Micah pulled through the gate and up the driveway, his heart gave a funny lurch. Sitting on his porch, still dressed in the same raggedy clothing but sporting a heavy green army jacket, was Muse. He didn't ask how she got there, how she had found a way through his security system. He had given up on asking her questions, always receiving cryptic and dismissive answers. She was there and he was grateful. It was all that mattered.

She didn't seem mad that he moved away from her, but she did make him pay. After telling him she had his third novel ready, she once again handed him a sheet of paper, and this time all that was written on it was a name and phone number. She told him to call the guy and explained what he needed to ask for. Micah's stomach twisted at the request, but he picked up the phone. Two hours later he was waiting in an alley behind the hospital, pacing by a door that read HOSPITAL PERSONNEL ONLY.

Bob came out on his break and lit a cigarette, looking around suspiciously before handing Micah a small wrapped bundle. Without a word, Micah handed him a wad of folded bills and it was over. Not a word was spoken between the two. Bob explained over the phone how he would obtain the objects, but it still didn't make Micah feel better as he drove home, glancing down at the horrible package that lay on the passenger seat. He hoped like hell he wouldn't get pulled over, knowing that if he did, despite his promises to the contrary, he would give Bob up in a heartbeat. *What kind of person was willing to do this sort of thing, anyways?*

When he walked in the door, Muse was waiting for him, the pile of stones and bones already arranged. He tried to hand her the bundle but she refused.

"Gotta be you."

Micah took a deep breath and set the bundle on the table, gingerly unwrapping the plastic. He nearly shrieked when he saw the little hands, despite already knowing what the package contained. The baby had been stillborn, its body on the way to be cremated, so at least he wasn't responsible for its death. He was glad that they weren't pink anymore, the way a newborn's hands should look, but it was still awful.

Chubby fingers the color of clay were clenched into tight fists, ending in bloody stumps at the wrist. They felt cool to the touch and still terribly soft. He turned his head to the side and vomited as he placed them on the pile, mindful not to get puke on the offering.

This time when he awoke, Muse was still seated at his table, eating ice cream directly from the carton. He stared at her in disbelief for a moment, willing her to disappear like a phantom.

She remained real and nasty, smacking her lips loudly as she shoveled spoonfuls of rocky road into her nearly toothless mouth.

"Shouldn't you be gone?" He knew he sounded cranky but didn't care. That wretched old witch had made him collect *baby hands* for her.

"Got nowhere to go. I'm moving in with you."

***

Micah took a cab from the airport, his mood darkening more with each mile he came closer to home. He figured at first that it wouldn't be so bad to have her there; he was gone most of the time anyway. Book signings and public appearances ate up a lot of his free time. He had no steady girlfriend, preferring one night stands with women he met at conventions and book club appearances. It was easier for him that way, and he knew deep inside that if he were to let a woman get too close to him, he might divulge his secret.

Micah thought it really wasn't that bad living with the crone at first. She didn't eat much and spent most of her time in her room. He would occasionally run into her in the kitchen, or hear her cackling laugh coming through the closed door as he walked down the hall. She seemed to enjoy sitcoms quite a bit, reruns of *Friends* entertained her for hours. For the most part she left him alone.

She stunk, though. Over the months her stink permeated every room of the house, musty and rank, it was an old lady smell. Though she now had access to a shower every day, she never changed her clothes and never appeared any cleaner. Every accidental glimpse of her, every time he smelled her sickly odor, every time he heard her laughs muffled behind the door, she reminded him of how far he was willing to go for success. She showed him just how dark he was inside, to what lengths he was capable of going and what depravities he would commit for the next tale.

It was late and Micah stayed quiet as he entered. He was relieved there was no sign of Muse and that her bedroom door was shut. Exhausted from the trip, he headed straight to his own bedroom on the opposite side of the house and disrobed, falling into bed without even a shower.

He knew that within a few days, it would be time to discuss the next book with her, and he wondered how long he could carry on with this. He didn't even want to think about what offerings would be requested after the baby hands, and despised the person he had become. With royalties from the movie getting ready to pour in, he seriously considered retiring and just investing the money he had already earned.

Maybe I'll take a job at one of the big publishers as an editor. Hell, maybe I'll start my own publishing company!

The ideas swirled through his head as he eventually fell into an uneasy sleep.

***

Micah plunged his hands into long hair, gently pressuring her to take his cock deeper into her throat. She didn't gag or protest; she sucked him in deep, causing his hips to involuntarily thrust harder. He moaned while she made greedy noises with her mouth, and he began to pump furiously against her face, close to the most powerful release of his life. As he came hard, she continued, not shying away from his semen like so many other women, but gobbling it down as if she couldn't get enough, he came again, surprising them both with the second burst.

As the spasms subsided and his heart rate began to decrease, Micah stroked her hair, realizing with a start that the tresses in his hand were no longer smooth and soft. His hands gripped the coarse and tangled mess, pulling her away from his cock and lifting her face to his own.

He let out a startled cry when Muse's wrinkled face came into view, her rotting teeth exposed in a lascivious smile while saliva and semen glistened on her creased chin. Trying to push her away, his arms lost strength and fell by his side, paralyzed. He watched in horror as she crawled up his prone body, her sagging tits dragging along his chest, horrible and deflated, the wrinkled skin splotched with age spots

"Ooooh Lover!" she cooed in her raspy voice. "My turn! But don't

worry, I hear the older the berry the sweeter the juice!"

Muse straddled his head and sat on his face.

***

Micah bolted upright in bed, a scream lodged painfully in his throat and his heart hammering in his chest. Early morning sunlight streamed through the blinds, momentarily blinding him. As his confusion subsided, he realized he was in his own bed. Alone. Breathing a sigh of relief, he ran a shaky hand through his hair and it came back wet with sweat. His hair wasn't the only thing wet; he realized with disgust that he had ejaculated during his dream.

That was some sick shit, he thought.

After a long shower, he stripped the soiled linens and dumped them in the washing machine with more detergent than necessary, before heading to the kitchen to make himself breakfast. As he cooked, he began to regain some sense of normalcy and he felt a strengthening of his convictions from the night before.

I can't go on like this. I need to stop it. Maybe I will start my own publishing company. With three bestsellers, two of which are still on the charts, and a major motion picture based off my last novel, I have plenty of money.

"Are you ready?" Muse's raspy voice startled him so badly that he dropped the spatula, his hand shaking when he bent to retrieve it.

She laughed, her eyes glittering like chips of black stone in her wizened face where she sat at the table.

"How long have you been there? I didn't hear you come in."

"Oh, for a while, boy. It's time to talk about your next book. I need another offering."

Micah stood in the kitchen looking at her for a long time, then dropped his eyes to the floor. *I can do this. I need to do this.*

"I've been thinking, Muse."

"Do tell, son." Her voice sounded amused.

"Well . . . " He paused for a moment, considering what to say, before continuing in a rush, his words flowing faster than he could think. "I don't want to do this anymore. I mean, I'm grateful for everything you have done for me, and we've had a good run at it. But I just think that it's time to stop this. I want to retire and start my own publishing company. I will pay you whatever you want for what you've done."

Micah looked up at her, not sure what he expected to see. Anger or maybe sadness, but she just smiled at him, her head cocked to the side.

"I see, boy." When she spoke, her voice was soft, but crackly. "That's too bad. Being a publisher is a respectable job, but I thought you wanted to be a writer. I thought you loved the life in the spotlight."

Muse rose with dignity, turning her back on him to walk to her bedroom. On the way, she called to him over her shoulder. "Too bad you can't do this after one more. This one was going to win awards." Then she disappeared into the bedroom, leaving the door open behind her.

Micah was stunned. He thought he had achieved everything he wanted in life with the first three books, but the promise of an award winning novel flashed through his head.

Award winning. He had done very well for himself, but had won no awards. *Now that would be something to end my career on*, he thought.

Hating himself for being curious, calling himself a fool for even letting her bait him into considering doing one more, he still felt pulled. He walked down the hall and stood just outside the doorway, his expression serious.

"What award?"

Muse sat upon the single bed, her bag of tricks on the floor between her loafers. She didn't have anything to pack, had brought nothing aside from the bag, no other clothing or possessions. Tilting her head to the side again and smiling slightly, she couldn't hide the triumph in her eyes.

"This one will win the Bram Stoker Award. It may even put you at the top of the game."

"What would I have to do?"

"You have to fuck me. But don't worry, boy. *The older the berry, the sweeter the juice.*" She cackled wildly.

Micah clenched his fists, a flood of anger making him want to pummel her face until there was nothing left. Muse only laughed harder.

"Ha Ha! I'm only kidding! It's nothing so awful as that! I'm too old to give a shit about your little prick anyways." She still snickered.

"So what do I have to do?"

"I need a heart. One you cut out yourself." Muse was all business now.

"Are you *crazy*, old woman?"

"Perhaps. But it's what I need. Now close your mouth; you look like an idiot." She leaned forward on the bed, her eyes bright with anticipation as she told him how it could be done. "There are hundreds of homeless in this town. People no one would ever miss. All you gotta do is get one to come home with you, promise him money or food or something. And when he's here—"

She clapped her hands together with a loud crack, and Micah jumped.

"I don't know. I can't kill someone." Micah felt ill, the whole conversation unreal. He had done some hard things over the last few years in pursuit of his dreams, but didn't think he was capable of cold-blooded murder.

Suddenly he wished more than anything he had never met Muse. He thought he'd give anything to go back to his lousy copy editor job, miserable but at least unaware of the depraved monster living within him. As much as he wanted to tell himself he wasn't a murderer, he knew the appeal of that award was *strong*, and was starting to have an idea of how he could achieve it. It was crazy to even consider, but he knew that he would follow through. He wanted that award.

"Okay," he said. "One more."

***

The heart was warm and slippery in his hands and he almost dropped it on the floor, imagining he could still feel it twitching in his hands. The knife hadn't been sharp enough to cut through the sternum, so he'd been left with no other choice than to cut the body nearly in half and get at it through the abdominal cavity. Even then, cutting through the thick vessels had been tough. He hadn't want to damage the heart itself, so he had to go slow, unable to clearly see what he was doing through the gore. Soaked in sweat and covered in blood and body fluids by the time he finished, he smelled like the backroom of a butcher shop.

Micah laid the heart gently upon the pile of stones and waited. Nothing happened. He thought he had arranged them in the proper order. He sighed heavily and scratched his forehead, leaving behind a gory streak at his temple.

Despite the snarl of rage frozen on her features and the shocked accusation in her vacant stare, she had been surprisingly easy to smother. Cutting her open had been horrendous, her insides smelled worse than her outside, and he accidentally punctured the large intestine, releasing the ripe odor of shit and digestion into the room. Her slime seemed to cover every inch of him, he could taste it in his mouth, but he had gotten the job done. But it hadn't worked! The stones just wouldn't smoke. He wished he knew the correct words to say, those foreign, guttural mutterings of Muse's. But he didn't. It wasn't going to work.

Micah walked into the kitchen with the intention of washing up a bit before considering what to do with her dismembered body, but stopped in his tracks. Micah flew into the other room and hauled Muse's smelly corpse over his shoulder, dragging her entrails behind him as he entered the office and dropped her in a broken heap next to the computer chair. Her glassy eyes stared at him as he drummed his bloody fingers on the desk, waiting for the computer to boot up. Everywhere he touched, he left smears of gore, but he didn't notice. He was caught up in the clarity of his task.

As the machine whirred to life, Micah sneered at the dead woman, visions of her hand jerking him off, dead kittens and the clenched fists of an infant, rolled through his memory. He placed his fingers on the keyboard as he worked a giant gob of snot up to the back of his throat. It felt hot and slippery in his mouth before he let it go, spitting the wad of green mucus into Muse's dead face with a *splat!*

He watched the chunky spit roll over the contours of her craggy face as his fingers battered the words across the screen. He didn't need to look at what he typed, he knew what they said.

Micah had all but given up on his dream of becoming a writer, he typed, *on the day that he met Muse.*

FLESH

THE MUSIC THUMPED LOUDLY over the crowded bar as Scott
took a stool, his eyes scanning the dance floor.

God I hate this techno shit, he thought, raising his chin slightly
and holding up one finger when the bartender appeared. He
exchanged a ten dollar bill for a fresh vodka tonic, indicating with
a shake of his head that the man could keep the change. He
turned his attention back to the dancers.

People gyrated with abandon, bumping into one another in
the limited space. Blue and red strobe lights flashed across them,
lending the crowd a surreal appearance and painting the scene
on the back of his eyes in small bursts like snapshots. Some of
the women had removed their tops, their lacy bras glowing under
the black light. Others wore shirts that revealed more than a bra,
sheer fabric glued with sweat to bare breasts. In tight pants and
short skirts they bounced and grinded, pulling the eyes of the
men standing on the fringes, their drinks gripped in sweaty
hands with cocks half stiff from the parade of flesh.

Sometimes a brave soul would wander into the fray, only to
have his advances rebuffed by the very women who had seemed
to be inviting him to join them with their lewd moves and *fuck
me* glances. It was a brutal sport.

Someone bumped his shoulder and Scott turned, his senses assaulted by strong perfume and sweat. The woman smiled, her eyes glassy and bloodshot.

"Sorry about that," she shouted over the music, the yeasty smell of beer heavy on her breath.

Scott nodded at her and looked away but she leaned in close, pressing her breasts against him. He felt her erect nipples poke against his arm.

"Hey. Wanna buy me a drink?" Another wave of beer breath.

"Not really." He grimaced.

"What? You a fag?" She might have been attractive were she sober and not wearing so much makeup, but she sneered in a way that emphasized her overly large mouth, and her running mascara made her eyes looked like two dark holes.

"Maybe."

"Well, fuck you, buddy." She staggered away, quickly swallowed up by the crowd.

Glancing down the length of the bar, he was just about to give up for the night when he saw her, sitting on a stool with her back to the dance floor. Same as always. Scott sipped his vodka and swiveled on his stool a bit so he could see her as he pretended to watch the dancers. He eyed her long, dark hair trailing straight down her back in sharp contrast to the spikey, gel-hardened bobs and asymmetrical cuts the other women wore. He admired the conservative outfit she wore. Not a sign of her breasts or lace were visible through her modest clothing. It was all up to Scott's imagination what lay beneath those billowy folds. And he'd spent many hours doing just that.

The first time Scott saw her, he knew she was the one. He had watched her for three nights now, and the feeling had only intensified, burning in his chest as he watched her sip her drink, oblivious to the crowd around her, her slender hands twirling the straw in her glass. He would have her. Tonight.

Scott watched with clenched fists as the muscular bartender leaned across the bar, saying something in her ear. The bend of the other man's lips as he smiled at the girl told Scott he was flirting, but she only stared back at him with those fathomless dark eyes, neither smiling nor speaking until the bartender shook his head and walked away. Scott watched as she turned her head in his direction, her face expressionless. His pulse raced as he looked away.

From the corner of his eye, Scott saw her stand to leave, weaving her way through the rowdy crowd. He played it cool, finishing his own drink at a leisurely pace. He knew where she was going.

Walking out into the parking lot, Scott lit a cigarette and leaned against the rough brick wall, taking a deep drag and holding it for a moment. He hated that all the bars had gone smoke free. He couldn't see the woman anywhere, but it didn't matter.

***

Scott drove past the unassuming, single-story house and parked down the block under an ancient maple tree that hung low to the ground. The car would be all but hidden. Punching in the dashboard lighter, he surveyed the quiet neighborhood. The knob popped out and he lit his cigarette, smoking it at a leisurely pace. It was foolish to rush. Rushing might make him careless, and he couldn't afford careless. Reaching into the glove box, he pulled out a pair of leather gloves and a mask he had bought in an S&M store in the city. He fit it snuggly over his skull, zipping the vertical zipper over the back of his head, leaving the horizontal one open across his lips. Scott liked the option of using his mouth. He also liked the terror it inspired in his victims. Reaching under the passenger seat, he retrieved a large hunting knife with a serrated blade. Looking at the digital clock on the dashboard, he saw it was a few minutes after one in the morning.

Time to rock 'n' roll.

He got out of the car and closed the door, careful to be quiet in the still night. Remaining in the safety of darkness beneath the tree, he scanned the street, paying particular attention to the neighboring houses. All were dark and silent. *Good.* Slipping on the mask and gloves, he crept out from under the tree and walked over to her house, keeping to the shadows. Tall hedges bordering the property assisted him in his stealth as he crept around to the back.

The garage was attached, and Scott had determined on a previous visit that it would be his best course of entry. There was a back door to the garage, but when he tried the knob, he found it locked. Using the sturdy handle on the knife, he punched a hole in one of the lower panes of glass in the door's window, hesitating to listen for sounds of alarm. When none ensued, he picked the remaining glass out of the frame and carefully reached through to unlock the door.

Scott crept through the garage to the door that went into the house, and grinned as the knob turned with a gentle twist. He pulled it open and peeked around the corner, seeing nothing but a dark kitchen. His shoes made soft noises on the linoleum. There was just enough moonlight through the windows for him to navigate by as he made his way into the living room. A sound from down the hall caught his attention and he froze, straining to track it.

Scott smiled when he realized she was singing. Soft and soulful, her song was interrupted by the sound of water splashing. She was in the tub. He pondered the situation. Usually when he broke in, the woman would already be in bed asleep, defenseless as he slid in next to her and placed the knife against her throat.

Should I wait until she goes to bed? I can't just walk in and take her from the tub, she'll be slippery and hard to hold onto. For the first time in a long while, he was unsure how to proceed. In the end, her haunting voice spurred him on.

Her bedroom was at the end of the hallway. A slash of light spilled into the hall from the master bathroom. Scott entered the bedroom, grateful for the thick carpet that masked the sound of his approach. He crept up to the bathroom door, which stood ajar. In the shadow of the room, he looked around the door frame, and felt a flood of relief when he saw her sitting in the tub with her back to him. If he stayed quiet enough, he might be able to watch while she bathed. Glancing around the dark room, he decided he would slip into the closet when she got out, and wait until she slept for his attack.

The woman lay slouched low in the tub, her body hidden by its high ceramic sides. All of her long, silky hair was pinned in a loose bun, and he could only see her profile. Her eyes were closed and beads of sweat gathered on her upper lip. The air above the bath shimmered with steam. The only sound was that of her body parting the water. She had quit singing and that pained him. As he watched, her mouth parted and she let out a breathy moan, making him wonder what her hands were doing beneath the water.

Scott held his breath as she sat up, affording him a side-view of one small, firm breast. The nipple was so pale it was almost indistinguishable from the rest of her white skin, which steamed from the heat of the water. She moaned again.

The woman let one arm slide over the edge of the tub, revealing pink scar tissue running in stripes all the way up to her shoulder. She reached to grab something on the floor. An old-fashioned straight razor lay on the bath mat, its blade open and gleaming in the light from the vanity. She grabbed it by the pearl handle, bringing it up to her lips for a reverent kiss. Sliding back down in the water, she raised her right leg to shave.

Scott contemplated her disfigurement, both repulsed and excited. He longed to run his hand over her skin, feel the texture of those scars. Perhaps leave a few marks of his own.

Similar marks ran the length of her leg, some straight down the shin while others curled around the calf. They varied in color from a pale pink to a deep angry red, shiny and vibrant against her paleness. Resting her foot on the edge, she held the razor to her skin and sighed, a breathy exhalation of pleasure.

Scott held his breath, caught up in the intimate moment as he watched her run the razor up her leg, the beginning of an erection stirring his crotch.

She used no gels or soaps. Laying the blade against a spot on her ankle, her knuckles turning white as she pressed, she broke the skin and cut a ribbon of flesh off her shin as she drew the razor upward, blood rolling down her calf and dripping into the bath.

What the fuck is she doing? Scott's stomach turned as she flayed off a perfect strip of her skin. Setting down the razor, she held the flap in front of her face, and with another heady moan, stuffed it into her mouth. Blood and sweat ran down her chin in a pink line.

Taking a step back, Scott bumped into something and gasped.

The woman's head snapped towards the door in surprise, her eyes narrowing as she continued to chew. Scott froze. *What the fuck is wrong with her eyes? I thought they were brown.*

Unable to move, Scott watched as she stood and stepped out of the tub, water running off her slender body and darkening the blue bath mat. For a moment they just stared at each other, he in the shadows, she in the light. Blood flowed down her wet shin and dripped onto the floor, but she didn't seem to notice. She smiled at Scott, her teeth pink with her own blood.

"Well, hello, lover. It's about time you showed up." The woman stepped toward him, her hand outstretched.

Scott stood his ground, the knife pointing outward at hip level as she came toward him. Glancing down at the blade, she wasn't deterred. Moving forward as if to embrace him, she allowed the knife to slide easily through her flesh, puncturing her side as if she were made of cream cheese, instead of flesh and bone.

She gasped with pleasure, her flesh seeming to suck at the knife as he pulled it out.

At the sound of her ecstatic moan, Scott's resolve fled. Any trace of an erection shriveled and his stomach cramped at the thought of her eating her own skin.

Crazy. Bitch is fucking crazy. I have to get out of here. He took two running steps toward the bedroom door, then his ankle connected with something solid on the floor and his arms shot out to keep his balance. Plunging forward anyway, he reached his left hand out to break his fall, conscious of the hunting knife in his right.

His head banged against something hard. The moment before everything went black he mused about still having his mask on; *At least I won't cut my head.*

***

Soft, beautiful singing tugged Scott from unconsciousness, the comfortable darkness that swaddled him in its grip. Coming back in layers, he noticed his ferocious headache first. Subtle light pushed against his closed lids, but even that was too much for his aching head. He tried to rub it, but found he was unable to move his arms or legs.

His eyes snapped open in alarm, which caused the throb in his head to double.

It took a moment to recognize his surroundings and he had a panicked second when he thought he had somehow blinded his peripheral vision. It all came back to him in a rush, the woman in the tub, the singing, and that he was still in her house wearing the mask.

No wonder I can only see straight ahead.

Her face appeared directly in front of his own and Scott pulled back, trying to get as far away as he could.

No longer wearing the dark brown contacts, her real eyes gleamed a brilliant yellow, the pupils black, reptilian slits. She smiled and smoothed a hand across his stomach, making him aware that the mask was all he wore. His wrists and ankles were bound to the posts of a massive bed.

"Good. You're finally awake. I was worried." She leaned in to kiss him, getting only leather when he turned his head.

"What *are* you?"

"Oh you poor thing, you really did hit your head pretty hard. It's okay if you're confused." She continued to run her hand across his body from chest to thigh, each pass coming closer to his groin. "I'm your lover, of course."

Scott felt helpless. Accustomed to being the predator, he shuddered at the feeling of being prey. All he felt now was an overwhelming need to escape. The light touch of her hand upon his cock made him jump, and his body broke out in gooseflesh.

"Let me go, lady. Please."

She tilted her head to the side, an impish grin at odds with her alien eyes. "Sometimes when I'm without a lover for too long, I have to pleasure myself. It's okay now. I have you to pleasure me."

Scott stared at the woman who stood with a wink and stretched, showing off her lithe body. Up close, Scott saw the pink scars that ran down her arms and legs and crossed her breasts and belly, the twisted, red scar tissue where she had walked into his hunting knife.

"Like what you see?" She preened, turning from side to side to give him the full view.

The knife gleamed in the overhead light as she retrieved it from the table, running her fingertip across the sharp edge. A bead of blood welled up on her thumb and she put it to her mouth, her eyes closed in rapture as her pink tongue flicked out to capture it.

"I love the foreplay." Laying the blade against her wrist, she slowly drew it up the length of her arm, peeling away an inch-wide slice of her skin.

Realizing her intent, Scott clamped his lips shut an instant before the strip of flesh mashed against his mouth, smearing it with blood.

"Hard to get, huh?" Her tone mild and pleasant, she grabbed his balls, squeezing and twisting in one swift motion.

Bright flashes of light overtook Scott's vision and he opened his mouth, unsure of whether he would scream, vomit, or both. With unnatural speed, the woman stuffed the wad of skin into his mouth and pushed up on his jaw, making it impossible for him to spit. A salty, coppery tang filled his mouth and he felt bile burn its way up his throat, threatening to choke him as he lay there helpless. Left with little choice, he swallowed the meat whole, knowing that to chew would mean choking on his own puke.

She cooed in his ear, flicking the blade of the knife lightly across one of his nipples and licking the corner of his mouth before he could turn away. Sitting back, her freakish eyes appraised the naked expanse of his body.

His balls still ached and his head throbbed. He didn't like the way that her eyes kept returning to his crotch.

"You crazy fucking bitch. I'm done playing now. Let me go or I'm gonna kill you!"

She stuffed something silky in his mouth (he thought it might be panties) then zipped the mask up tight. "I think you've said enough."

"I was hoping you would be the one. It's been so long." She grabbed a scrapbook from the darkness beneath the bed, opening the cover and smiling at what she saw. Holding it above him so he could see, she pointed to various articles, lovingly snipped and pasted to the pages. She read aloud. "*City terrorized as masked rapist strikes again. Masked Menace claims his fourth victim. Citizens urged to watch over young, female neighbors as serial rapist remains at large.*"

Her hand returned to tracing his chest, the knife sliding lightly just behind it. Reaching a spot on his ribs, she pursed her mouth and cocked her head, then she nodded to herself in a satisfied way.

"Oh lover." She breathed, her face taking on a dreamy look. "Can you feel that? It's so sensual, isn't it? The sharing of flesh and pleasure. I'm inside you now."

Pausing to lift the book once again, she flipped to the back, a look of pride lighting her face as she showed him another set of articles.

"See, I'm in here too! *Yet another body found in the James River, missing its skin. Man's skinned corpse left beneath overpass. Police seeking leads in fifth slaying, sources calling the killer THE GHOUL.*" Laying the scrap book aside, she turned her attention back to Scott.

Kissing the zipper that covered Scott's mouth, she slashed with the knife, ignoring his muffled screams as his eyes bulged out in terror. Cutting away a section of the skin along his ribs, she paid no attention as he wailed and bucked when the knife hit bone.

His peripheral vision behind the mask shrank down to pinpoints as Scott began to black out again, barely seeing the dripping hunk of his flesh she held up before him.

"I'm in you now, lover." She said with a sigh, bringing his bloody flesh to his mouth and unzipping the mask. "Don't worry, lover. It's an acquired taste."

CARNALITY

CHAD KICKED AN EMPTY beer can into the gutter, listening as it rattled into the shadows. It was late, and he'd wandered farther than he'd meant to. Rows of dilapidated apartments interspersed with run-down shops rose up on either side of him. Normally he would've driven through this area with his windows up and doors locked. The street looked abandoned, but he knew dangers could be waiting for him. Gang bangers with nothing better to do than mug and beat the shit out of a white guy who'd wandered too far across the tracks, to name one. Maybe even kill him.

Chad didn't give a shit about that now. Shoving his hands into his pockets, he kept walking. He wasn't sober, but wasn't as drunk as he would like to have been, either. A saner part of his mind tried to reason with him. *You should've stayed at the bar with Elliot and Sasha. You can still find your way back before you get your dumb ass killed.*

"Fuck Elliot." He said to the empty street. "And fuck Sasha, too."

That was the whole problem. It was the reason he'd left the bar in the first place. His best friend in the world was too distracted with Sasha to notice his departure. Chad left them in the bar, swaying in each other's arms on the dance floor.

Chad left because he couldn't fuck Sasha. Not anymore. In two days she would become Mrs. Elliot Holmes, and she had ended her and Chad's affair last night.

"Fuck you Sasha." Chad repeated, but the words came out softer, as his rage turned to self-pity.

Finding a rusty bench next to an overflowing garbage can stinking like rot, Chad slumped down and put his head in his hands. He should hate Elliot, *wanted* to hate Elliot, but he just couldn't. They'd been friends since childhood, and in all those years, Elliot had never shown himself to be anything other than a great guy. They'd spent holidays with each other's families and vacationed together every summer since grade school. They'd gone to the same law school both their fathers had attended together decades before. Their families were intertwined in more ways than they were not. Elliot never once tried to take a girl from Chad, though Lord knows he could've had them all. Chad couldn't not *love* him.

It was Sasha who'd fucked things up. He had wanted her from the moment Elliot introduced them. He found her beautiful and vivacious, with a contagious spirit that made him want her constantly. But she belonged to Chad. He couldn't make a move on his best friend's girl.

At first, Chad had just been in awe of this amazing woman and his lucky friend who had found her. He couldn't even be jealous of Elliot, knowing in his heart that his friend deserved this divine creature.

They went everywhere together, the three of them inseparable. Sometimes Chad would bring a date as well, but it always felt wrong to include another woman, and he would find some excuse not to invite her out again.

Chad began to measure all potential girlfriends against Sasha, with the other girl coming up short every time.

He wanted Sasha. In fact, he wanted her more than he'd ever wanted anyone. Sometimes, he felt *sick* with need when she smiled at him, desperate to hear the sounds she would make as he slipped inside of her. His fantasies consumed his waking moments. But still, he had no intentions of betraying Elliot. He couldn't dream of hurting someone who trusted him so much.

Things could have been all right, despite Chad's desperate longing, but Sasha wouldn't let it lie. She knew Chad wanted her and she enjoyed the torment he felt. She began egging him on. Small things at first, like holding his gaze when he looked at her, or making sure her hand brushed his as they walked into the bar. Affectionate pats on the leg that started at the knee, but soon traveled up to his thigh. When the opportunity to consummate the relationship finally arrived, he'd accepted without hesitation.

She had driven him crazy. Sasha, with her big *fuck me* eyes and the need to know that every guy in the world desired her. It wasn't enough that she had Elliot, who was successful and handsome enough to catch the eyes of most women he met. Chad figured she really did love Elliot, but she needed more than what just one guy could give her. Maybe her daddy had been too distant, maybe mommy had shown her love with gifts rather than affection, blah, blah, blah.

Maybe she was just a slut.

It shouldn't matter. She was Elliot's problem. Chad had felt a mixture of relief and remorse when she'd told him last night they couldn't see each other anymore, that she wanted to try to be a good wife. He wanted her to be good to Elliot, and it killed him a little inside every time they fucked around behind his friend's back, but he would miss the sex.

"Fuck you, Sasha."

***

Chad stood up from the bench. His eyes scanned the shadows for movement, hyper-aware of his expensive clothes and the cash bulging in his wallet. Sobered, he gathered his bearings and turned back the way he came. He considered calling a cab, but figured he couldn't be too far from where he'd left his car.

After several blocks, Chad came across a small storefront, its lights shining out of a dirty front window adorned with a painted sign that read "Pawnshop." Looking at his watch, he saw it was going on midnight, but a sign on the door indicated that it was open.

What the fuck? This wasn't here before. He stopped to peer in the window, but the filth made it hard to see what was within.

Chad tried the door, certain it would be locked, that someone just forgot to flip the sign, but it opened easily. A bell tinkled as he walked in, announcing his arrival to an empty front desk.

"Hello? Is there anyone here?" Chad looked around at piles of junk stacked on shelves and the floor. A heap of jewelry lay scattered across broken toys; tools were mixed with kitchen wares. It would be impossible for the owner to know what he had in inventory. A thief's wet dream, if any of the shit was even worth anything.

"Just a moment." A frail voice called out from behind a room-length curtain that divided the shop from the back.

Chad picked up a balloon-like object that resembled a hot water bottle made of heavy, discolored rubber, with an unusual nozzle attached to a long hose that disappeared into the neck.

"Douche bag." A man's voice said, directly behind him. Startled from his inspection, Chad whirled around, and dropped the balloon. It landed on the concrete floor with a slap.

"Excuse me?" Chad said, offended.

"It's a douche bag."

Chad wiped his hand on his pant leg in disgust. "Who the hell would want a *used* douche bag?" Chad asked.

"You would be surprised what people come in here looking for. I don't judge." The old man winked at Chad and made his way across the floor slowly, settling on a stool behind the desk. "What can I help you with?"

"Me? Nothing, I guess. I just saw you were open and thought I'd check the place out. Why are you open so late?"

"My hours are never set, a perk of owning the place. I also suffer from insomnia something terrible lately. What can I show you?"

The old man leaned his elbows on the table. His eyes, like dark chips of glass, sparkled in his wizened face. Frizzy white hair formed a halo around his spotted head and his skin was dark. The man's shrewd gaze bored through Chad, making it hard to maintain eye contact.

"I don't need anything. Like I said, I just happened upon the place . . . "

"Everyone needs something, son. Sometimes we just don't know what it is." The man retrieved a gnarled looking pipe from a drawer, filling the bowl with dark, oily looking tobacco from a dish on the desk. As he smoked, the room filled with an acrid, sweet smell that made Chad's head swim, bringing back his drunk with a rush.

"You got troubles, boy. It's written all over your face."

Chad opened his mouth in denial, ready to flee back onto the street, away from the strange shop and the stranger old man with his trinkets and used feminine hygiene products. Instead, he found himself confessing. It all came out in a rush. The old guy just sat and smoked, nodding encouragement as the tale unraveled from their childhood friendship to their high school hijinks. The man passed no judgment as Chad admitted to his life-long jealousy of Elliot, and the way he had lived in his best friend's shadow for so many years.

When Chad got to the part about Sasha, he ranted at the old man about how the first time, when Elliot was passed out in the bedroom, Sasha had kissed him before stripping right there in the living room and riding him to a shrieking climax on the couch. His fists balled at his sides when he told of how she would taunt him, laughing no matter how hard he pounded himself into her, urging him to hurt her, loving the roughness she couldn't get from Elliot.

He ended his rant with his head hung as he muttered that he was supposed to throw Elliot a bachelor party tomorrow night, but couldn't even do that since Sasha insisted on tagging along.

For a moment neither spoke, Chad caught up in his misery, the old man smoking his pipe and nodding. Then he spoke, his voice raspy from the cloying tobacco that stung Chad's eyes.

"Pussy will destroy your life, son."

Chad glanced up.

"Yeah. I guess it can." He looked at the man, searching for some trace of humor or anger in his dark eyes, but saw only a weary sort of compassion that spoke of bitter experience.

"I don't know what to do."

"You could tell your friend. Come clean, and stop the wedding."

"I can't do that. It would break his heart."

"Better to break a heart now, than after he's already married the bitch."

"I know. But . . . "

"But you don't want to lose your friend."

"Right."

The old man nodded again, placing the hot pipe on the counter and pulling open a drawer, rummaging around as he spoke. "You have some tough choices, boy. Every man does sooner or later. But I think I've figured out what you need, and if I'm correct, it's right here." He held up a piece of paper, his wrinkled face bright with triumph. Laying the paper on the counter, he slid it towards Chad with one shaking hand.

It was some sort of ticket, a couple of inches long and maybe one inch wide, made of heavy card stock. The edges were worn and it was creased in places, the words printed on it faded but still legible. CLUB CARNAL.

"What is it?" He turned it over, seeing the words ADMIT TWO scrawled on the back.

"What does it look like? It's a ticket to Club Carnal." The man began to fill his pipe once again.

"What's Club Carnal? I've never even heard of it."

"Son, there are a great many things you've never heard of, and if you live as long as I have, there will *still* be mysteries in the world."

"So what is it? A strip club, or something?"

"Or something." The man said, his pipe once again full and trickling bluish smoke that wreathed his head.

Chad was growing annoyed by the old man and his enigmatic

speech. "Look, no offense man, I appreciate you letting me come in here and unload my troubles all over you like that, but I'm not going to pay money for an old ticket to a club I've never heard of."

"Who said anything about money? Consider it a gift. From an old man who's been there." His eyes sparkled, intense and unsettling.

"What's there?" Chad looked at the ticket in his hand, feeling uneasy about the exchange.

"A lesson. Maybe a hard one, but one you need to learn."

"That pussy will ruin my life?" Chad guessed.

"Exactly." The old man didn't smile.

"Where is Club Carnal?"

"The address is on the back."

Chad turned the stub over again and saw an address where before there had only been ADMIT TWO. 122 ½ E. Maple Street, written in spiky handwriting. He was sure it hadn't been there before.

"What the fuck? Is this some sort of trick?"

"Go there. See what there is to see and have fun. Fuck the girls, but whatever you do . . . " He paused, his flinty eyes piercing Chad's for emphasis. "Don't partake of the flesh. You will want to, but don't. Learn the lesson, son. Men are more susceptible to their sexual desires. It's about self-control. Don't take what is offered without question. No matter how much you want it. All of life has consequences, and beauty is never what it seems. Learn the lesson, Chad."

He gave Chad another hard look before sliding off his stool and disappearing back behind the curtain.

"Hey! What the hell does that even mean?" Chad called to his back.

If the old man heard Chad from behind the curtain, he gave no indication. Chad made it back onto the street before it even occurred to him that he'd never given the other man his name.

***

Maple Street was in the old section of town, a few blocks away from the strange little shop. Knowing he should just find his car and go home, he turned down the deserted sidewalk to where it intersected Maple instead. He doubted Club Carnal even existed, since he'd never heard anyone mention the place. It wouldn't hurt to check though.

"You looking for a date?"

The voice startled Chad. Turning, he could make out the figure of a woman standing in the deep shadows of a doorway. When he didn't reply, she stepped out into the light cast by a street lamp. She was pretty in a tired sort of way, still young enough to have retained her sex appeal despite the lines etched around her eyes and mouth. If she was a junkie, it didn't show yet. Her figure was full in the right places, her body not yet reduced to the cadaverous stature of someone who has handed the reins of her life over to drugs.

"Actually, I'm looking for a place called Club Carnal."

"Never heard of it." She took the ticket from his outstretched hand and angled it towards the light, her brow furrowed as she squinted to read the handwriting on the back. Handing it back to him, she shrugged. "Sorry."

"Thanks anyway." Chad smiled and turned to walk away then changed his mind. "You want to come with?"

"Like a date?" She opened her eyes wide with feigned innocence, though the corner of her mouth quirked up in the start of a sarcastic smile.

"Maybe. Just to see what's there. I mean, really, it's not like there's a line of *dates* here on the street."

She shrugged and stepped up beside him on the walk.

"My name's Lily. You aren't some kind of serial killer, are you?"

"Chad." He accepted her gentle handshake, liking the way her slender hand felt in his own. "And no, I'm not any kind of killer. But I probably wouldn't tell you the truth if I was, you know".

Up close, he saw she was younger than he'd guessed. Probably in her early twenties. She was braless under a deeply cut shirt that clung to her full breasts and ended at a skirt so short it could practically pass for a belt. Though he was average height, he figured she would have to crane her neck to look up at him without the stiletto boots she wore.

"So what do you do?" She asked as they walked, her head turned toward him, watching his every move.

Chad's mind swam, trying to come up with a believable lie, wondering about the wisdom of telling her his occupation. What if it was a set-up? He was filled with visions of some pimp following at a distance, sneaking up to conk him on the head and roll him.

Oh come on! Chad thought, shaking his head at his own folly. *You are walking down a dark, deserted street in the company of a hooker you just met, looking for a club that probably doesn't exist on recommendation of some creepy old bastard in a run-down pawn shop that sells douche bags in the middle of the night. And now you want to start thinking about what is or isn't prudent?*

"I'm a lawyer."

"That's cool. Maybe I'll take your card. Might need you some day." Lily laughed, a husky sound Chad enjoyed.

"Sorry, I only do family law."

"Good one," she replied, grinning. "I'll have to remember that."

"Can I ask you a question?" Chad said.

"Probably not." She said with a sigh. "But you will, anyway."

"Why do you do it?"

"Do what?" She cocked her head to the side.

"You know. What you do for a living." Chad resisted the urge to kick at the ground like a boy on the schoolyard. Somewhere between that shadowy doorway and their short banter, he'd begun to like Lily.

"What? Being a hooker? It's okay. I know what I am." Lily tipped her head back and looked at the stars. "I guess it's just something I fell into. My Mom died when I was young and I was on my own at fifteen. I could go on and on with my sad story, but the truth is, it pays the bills. And it's a hell of a lot better than waitressing for quarter tips."

"I'm sorry that happened to you." Chad's apology felt inadequate, and he felt guilty about his comparably privileged life.

"Not your fault. We all have our problems. Hey look. We're here."

They stopped in front of a low brick building, the windows covered by boards. It looked to have been closed up for a while, and Chad couldn't immediately tell what sort of business it had housed when open. Glancing up and down the street, he saw that more businesses were boarded up than not.

"Well, this is 122, but I don't see a 122 ½. Usually it would be an apartment above the actual business in a place like this, but there's only one floor. I guess it doesn't exist." He was a little pissed at the old man for sending him on a wild goose chase, but at least Lily's company had been nice.

"Maybe it's down there?" Lily pointed down a narrow alley south of the building which was barely wide enough to let them enter side by side.

"I suppose it could be. You want to check it out?"

"I don't know."

"Come on. If it's not there, we'll come right back out. And if it is, I'll buy you a drink."

"You'd owe me more than one drink for going down that creepy alley."

"Okay, I'll buy you as many drinks as you want." He held out a hand to her, grinning in the most disarming way he could when she didn't take it. "It's okay. I'll protect you."

Lily snorted, her eyebrows raised as she made a show of looking him up and down, clearly not reassured by his fancy clothes and lean build.

Chad laughed and shrugged, pulling his hand back.

"We'll be a team. If someone attacks us, I'll distract them while you take off one of those high heels and stab them with it."

"I'll go down there with you on one condition. If we don't find anything, you walk me back to my place and pay for a date."

"That sounds fair. If we don't find anything, I might just want that date after all." Chad winked and held his hand out again, and after only a moment of hesitation, Lily took it.

***

The light from the street barely illuminated the narrow alley and they had to proceed slowly to keep from tripping over trash that littered the ground. A heavy stink of urine and garbage made them breathe through their mouths, and Chad had to squeeze Lily's hand to keep her from fleeing when a rat squeaked at them from atop a pile of refuse. Chad was about to give up and turn around when the thump of heavy bass reached him, more a feeling than a sound. A few yards down, they came upon the door.

Set flush with the brick, the heavy steel door was huge, easily twice the size of an average one, with no discernible knob or handle. Spray painted in black letters across it were two words: CLUB CARNAL. The music came from behind the door.

Looking over his shoulder at Lily, Chad raised his eyebrows in question. She shrugged, squeezing his hand lightly. He raised his other fist and rapped on the door, expecting a hollow gonging noise to reverberate down the alley, but hearing only a soft knock. After several moments he turned to Lily.

"There's no way anyone will hear us knocking over that music. Maybe there's another way in."

The door squealed on unseen hinges as it opened inward, revealing a man in a stained white t-shirt and snug jeans with homemade tattoos covering nearly every inch of exposed skin, including his face and neck. Ignoring Chad and Lily, the guy leaned out and surveyed the alley with narrowed eyes, before allowing them to enter.

Inside it was dark, the only illumination coming from a black light that caused neon graffiti on the walls to glow crude etchings and misspelled words that shocked the eyes in day-glow pinks, greens and yellows. The music was loud and heavy.

Turning toward Chad, the big man said nothing, just held out a scarred hand, eyebrows raised.

"Oh yeah." Chad said, his voice swallowed up by the beat as he patted first one pocket, then the other with a frantic certainty he had lost the ticket and they would be thrown back out into the alley with the rats and garbage. He jumped when Lily slid her small hand into his front pocket, her fingertips grazing his balls as she retrieved the ticket deep within and laid it in the bouncer's palm. She winked at Chad as they waited for the man to inspect the stub.

Satisfied with what he saw, the guy opened an interior door and ushered them past the entrance.

Chad's first impression of Club Carnal was one of sensory overload as he tried to take in all the sights and sounds at once. It was much louder than he would have imagined from the alley. The music vibrated in his chest, and was occasionally punctuated by shrill laughter and screams. The dance floor was full of gyrating bodies in various states of undress. Both women and men danced on raised platforms, their nude bodies glowing with neon paint like that which adorned the walls in the entry. A recessed area contained circular booths where couples and whole groups of people lounged, some engaged in sex acts while others smoked hookahs made of brightly colored glass, the bluish smoke creating a haze that fell upon the room like mist.

Lily pulled on Chad's arm, her mouth close to his ear so he would hear her shout.

"No way this place is legal."

He nodded, then smiled when he saw the look of awe that had transformed her face into that of a little girl's. The strobe lights made her pale skin look bluish, then green, as her mascara ringed eyes scanned the room, wide with wonder.

A pretty young woman holding an empty tray walked up to them, clad only in a loincloth, her nipples dusted with glitter and sporting clamps from which small peacock feathers hung. She grabbed Lily by the hand and led her away as Chad hurried to keep up, taking them to an empty booth that held a translucent pink hookah and a dish of sticky looking tobacco. The waitress disappeared without a word, only to return moments later with her tray full of drinks in carnival colors which she arranged before the two of them.

Fumbling with his wallet, unsure of the price of the drinks he hadn't ordered, Chad pulled out two twenties, which the woman tucked into the strip of leather holding the loincloth in place. She handed them each one of the mouthpieces attached to the pipe, then leaned over and lit it for them, giving Chad a full view of her bare crotch beneath the cloth.

Lily put the tube in her mouth, breathed deeply, and held the smoke, a dreamy expression taking over her face as she exhaled. Even in the sporadic light from the dance floor, Chad watched as her pupils grew large and glassy.

Must be some good shit, he thought, his own mouthpiece still in hand as he weighed the wisdom of smoking an unknown drug in an illegal club deep within the city. He already felt strange, probably from breathing the second-hand haze that enveloped the room. In the end he gave in, took a deep drag, and felt euphoria wash over him in waves.

Is it hash? Opium? The world became soft at the edges, and his whole body thrummed like a tuning fork.

***

Somehow the drinks on the table were half empty, and Lily was on his lap, her mouth tasting of fruit and bitter alcohol as she pressed it sloppily against his own.

The low-cut shirt was rent down the middle, her bare breasts filling his hands. He looked down at them, unsure how they had gotten in this position, and noticed that each nipple was tattooed with a rose. That had to have hurt like hell, he thought, then giggled, pinching first one, then the other, much too hard. Lily moaned and shoved her wet tongue into his ear. Chad took another hit from the hookah.

The glasses were empty now, and Chad leaned back on the bench, pants around his knees. Lily dragged her teeth up the underside of his cock, causing him to groan. It should've hurt, but everything felt wonderful and electric. His head spun as she sucked at him, his eyes trying to focus on the people around them. In the next booth, a fat businessman lay sprawled while a blonde bounced on his face, squealing each time she landed. A threesome was happening on the floor at his feet, though he had a hard time concentrating enough to figure out the players, and who was doing what to whom. The whole room was alive with writhing bodies, the smell of sex mingling with the sweet smell of smoke.

The music stopped and the voice of the DJ boomed over the crowd.

"The spoons!"

The waitress returned with a silver object in her hand. It looked like a large melon-baller to Chad, the edges wickedly sharp. She set it on the table and pushed between them, pressing Lily back into the bench with a hungry kiss, her ass in Chad's face. He reached out to trace the lines of her vulva, his finger sliding between the slick folds of flesh with ease as he rose up to his knees, almost falling over on shaky legs. Lily groaned as the waitress buried her face between her thighs and growled, her eyes glazed, a dazed expression on her face. The whole room seemed to tilt, but Chad welcomed the shift. It felt like his whole body was fluid and fire with bolts of pleasure shooting out from his groin as he slid his cock into the woman.

The waitress glanced over her shoulder and grinned, a savage look on her face. For a moment, it seemed the flesh on it blurred into something demonic, skeletal and cruel, visible for only a second before she returned her attention to Lily. Chad shuddered but continued on, pumping for all his worth, not bothering to look at the stranger who slipped one thick, spit-slick finger between his cheeks to circle his asshole. He came with a roar and fell back against the cushion, watching the scene with pleasant exhaustion.

The waitress sat up, pulling Lily with her so the three of them were thigh to thigh on the bench. Without a word, she retrieved the odd spoon from the table, scraped it down the inside of her leg. Chad shook his head to clear it, watching in open-mouthed awe as the young woman scooped a chunk of flesh from her leg with a smile, offering it to Lily's waiting mouth. The wound was bloodless, as if she were made of pale clay instead of flesh and bone, a pale, golden light revealed beneath her skin.

Lily swallowed with a sigh of pleasure, her eyes glowing with the same amber light as she looked across the woman to Chad, her mouth slack.

Chad shook his head again. This shit was crazy, but it didn't seem quite as wrong as it should. Somewhere in the back of his mind an alarm sounded, and an old man's voice screeched something about not partaking of the flesh, but he ignored it, accepting a smooth chunk from the woman's belly with all the reverence of an alter boy's first communion.

The taste exploded across his tongue, sweet like honey and musky. Like nothing he had tasted before, filling his whole being with need.

He wanted more, and she obliged, the spoon dipping over and over, the offering of her flesh disappearing into their mouths with increasing speed.

Chad couldn't get enough, the warmth inside his body felt like living light and danced across his every nerve, ending in orgasmic intensity. When the woman stood and pressed the spoon, still remarkably cool despite her touch, into his hand, he knew what was expected of him and turned to Lily.

His entire world shrank down to just this moment, this booth, and Lily's soft body. He wanted to cut a new entrance in her, one that no other man had ever used.

They squirmed against one another, making and breaking connections at the mouth and crotch, nothing existed but fingers and tongues and his cock as he carved at her flesh. It came away easily, like ice cream, like butter, and they both consumed it greedily as the rest of the room retreated, until there was nothing more than moans and whispers and the liquid sounds of sucking and fucking and carnal bliss.

Throwing the spoon down with impatience, Chad attacked her with his mouth, biting and chewing as Lily's squeals of delight joined the chorus of physical pleasure.

***

A shrill train whistle blew and afternoon sunlight stabbed his eyes, threatening to make Chad's head explode as he awoke on a rough concrete floor. The throbbing in his head was so intense he felt nauseated.

He slowly sat up in a room he didn't recognize. He was naked from the waist down, and his cock felt raw and abused. His mouth was dry, and there was a coppery taste in it that made his stomach churn. He rolled onto his side just in time to unleash a stream of bitter vomit onto the floor.

Lying in misery as his heaving gut calmed, Chad struggled to remember the night before, bits and pieces of memory causing his head to spin. He recalled a hooker. Lily? And some sort of club. It all came rushing back in a flood, causing him to bolt upright in another nauseating wave of pain.

"Oh shit," he groaned, gathering his bearings as his head continued to spin. He was in what seemed to be a long-abandoned building. The floors were heaped with trash and dirt, and the windows were boarded over, the glass long gone. A train whistle sounded again, making him think he was near the railroad yard.

But that was impossible. He'd been on Maple, and that was miles away from the railroad. Chad squinted to inspect the shadows around him, and realized he wasn't alone. A naked woman lay a few feet away, her narrow back to him.

"Lily? Is that you?"

The woman didn't reply.

With sinking dread, Chad pulled his pants up and buckled his belt, crawling across the rough floor to where she lay, unmoving.

"Are you okay?"

Chad prodded her shoulder. As he touched her cold skin, a voice jabbered incoherently in his head, and he knew before he rolled her over that she would be dead. She flopped onto her back and Chad screamed, a high-pitched sound that echoed back to him as he fell on his ass. Rocks and glass gouged his palms as he scuttled crab-like away from the body.

All of one breast and much of her thighs were gone, exposing raw, red tissue and gleaming bone. Her abdomen had been clawed open, her dull, useless organs drying in the air. In some places he could see where the tool had cut away the flesh clean, but other places looked gnawed on, the edges rough and *chewed*.

Lily's face had not been spared the ravaging, as her lips and much of the surrounding cheeks were torn away, leaving the tendons and fascia beneath.

Her blue eyes stared off, the film of death already formed upon them, and her bloody teeth seemed to sneer at him, blaming him for what had happened to her. As Chad watched, a fat black fly landed on the surface of one eyeball and began to crawl around.

He puked again, this time not stopping until each heave produced only a foamy stream of dark, bitter bile. But even as he retched, memories of the club assailed him and he felt a longing to be back, to immerse himself in that pure bliss one more time. His groin tingled with anticipation. He spit in the dust, trying to get the taste from his mouth.

I killed her. I fucking killed her. Chad thought, his head cradled in his hands as hot tears flooded his eyes. *And I fucking* ate *her.*

Chad's stomach churned again and he splattered his shoes with a fresh bout of acid, surprised there was anything left in him. He wasn't entirely shocked to realize he was half hard from the memories.

Panic rose to gnaw at his chest, his heart pounding furiously as he considered what he should do. He was in an abandoned building, next to the corpse of a hooker he'd killed and eaten, far from his home and car. He half expected to hear the whine of sirens and the banging of cops at the door, as if his guilt was being broadcast through the atmosphere and straight to the nearest station.

"Calm down." Chad said, trying hard to make his body obey, his pulse still racing. "You're a lawyer. You know about crime. Look at this as a crime scene."

Taking several deep breaths, Chad closed his eyes and counted to ten. When he opened them, he tried to survey the scene with a critical eye, letting the voice of his law experience speak in his mind.

First problem, DNA from his saliva, semen, and god knew what else.

It's okay. The voice reasoned. *Your record is clean. They won't have your DNA on file. Besides, if you're lucky, she won't be found.*

Witnesses.

Everyone at the club was engaged in one or more illegal activities. They won't be volunteering anything. The street was abandoned during your walk. No one knew you. If anyone saw you, you won't know unless they come forward, but in that section of town, people don't trust the cops.

Did I leave anything behind? He began to check his pockets and wallet.

Keys. Phone. Driver's License. Credit Cards. Cash. Looks like it's all there.

How to get home.

Walk. Not too fast, not too slow. Do nothing to attract attention. When you get to a better area of town, you can call a cab and go home. Throw your clothes and shoes in the trash compactor. Shower and shave and act like none of this ever happened.

Chad looked at Lily, discarded on the floor like trash. He felt bad. He hadn't meant to hurt her, but right now the fact that she was a hooker was his biggest break. Even if the cops found her body soon, they probably wouldn't put too many resources into finding her killer without a family breathing down their necks. He felt like a bastard, but was grateful she was one of the city's disposable souls.

"I'm sorry, Lily." He turned away but stopped when something caught his eye. Her hand gripped a piece of paper. His heart began to pound once again, making him dizzy with the thought of how he had almost left behind the one clue that could link him to the scene. Careful not to touch her, he pried the paper from her grip. It was exactly what he had feared, the ticket stub the old man at the pawn shop had given him.

Turning it over in his hand, Chad saw the address on the back now read 311 ¼ Oxford Drive, though the creases seemed to be in the same places, and the wear made it look identical to the other.

Hell, that's almost in my neighborhood.

Chad's phone vibrated in his pocket, startling him, and he dropped the ticket. Grabbing the phone, he looked at the caller ID. It was Elliot. He flipped the phone open.

"Elliot . . . "

"Hey man! What the hell happened to you last night?" Elliot's voice was loud as usual, full of enthusiasm.

"Sorry, Elliot. I didn't mean to ditch on you like that. I wasn't feeling very well."

"Sure. Sure. You met some little hottie while we were dancing and left with her, didn't you?"

"No." Chad glanced at Lily, and feelings of disgust and desire warred within him, causing him to shudder. "It wasn't a woman. Listen, Elliot. Now really isn't the best . . . "

"Sasha wants me to ask you if we're still on for tonight?"

Chad bent to retrieve the fallen ticket, his mind barely on the conversation.

"Tonight?"

"Yeah. The bachelor party. You know. The one you're supposed to be throwing your best friend."

"I don't know, man. Something's come up—"

"Chad, you can't back out on us now. Sasha's hoping you're going to take us to a strip club. Maybe one of the really sleazy ones on the East Side." Elliot chuckled, and Chad could imagine him winking at Sasha in the background.

Turning the ticket over, Chad stared at the new address, realizing it wasn't the only thing that had changed. Visions of Lily and the woman last night flooded his mind, quickly replaced by memories of him and Sasha fucking like animals on the couch while Elliot slept in the next room. He thought of how cold Sasha had been when she broke it off with him. He thought of how much Elliot meant to him and the heartbreak he would suffer when he learned what a slut his new wife really was. He imagined the two of them fucking her at the same time in a sticky booth at Club Carnal. Then he thought of the spoons and a room full of people, taking out their most primal desires on one another.

He knew what he needed to do. He *wanted* to do it for Elliot, after what Sasha had done to him, but mostly he wanted to be back there just one more time. One more night of unearthly bliss and he could save his best pal from what would only result in a nasty divorce.

"Yeah, Elliot. We're still on. But it won't be some cheap strip club for *my* best friend and his fiancé."

Chad looked at the scribbled handwriting on the back of the stub. ADMIT THREE.

"I have somewhere much better in mind."

LUNCH DATE WITH LOA LOA

"**M**R. HANKS? DR. MCDONALD will see you now."

"Thank you." Mark stood up from his seat, tossing a well-worn copy of *National Geographic* onto the waiting room's coffee table. Following the pretty, blonde nurse, he wondered if she would be impressed if she knew he had taken some of the pictures in that magazine.

I doubt it, he thought, thanking her once again when she showed him into an exam room. Ordinarily he would have taken the chance and brought it up anyway, but he was too preoccupied for any attempt at flirtation.

Another nurse knocked before entering, this one much older and far less attractive, her salt and pepper hair cropped short and her face cast into a permanent frown.

"Please roll up your shirt sleeve, Mr. Hanks." She stuck a thermometer in his mouth, then strapped the blood pressure cuff around his bicep and pumped it brutally tight, her fingers pressed firmly on his inner wrist.

"So what brings you in today, Mr. Hanks?"

"Dere's a womb in ma aye." He muttered around the thermometer.

"I'm sorry, what?" She released the cuff and scratched some

numbers on a pad of paper, finally glancing at Mark, who raised his eyebrows and pointed at his mouth with his free hand.

"Yes, of course." She removed the thermometer and held up a finger to prevent him from speaking as she scratched more numbers down. "Now what were you saying?"

"There's a worm in my eye." Though his tone was calm, Mark's insides twisted just saying it.

"A worm in your eye." The nurse frowned.

"Yeah."

"Any other symptoms?"

Mark thought about it for a moment before answering, doing a mental inventory of his body. "Some soreness in my joints, a rash that comes and goes, and a lot of pain in my eye when it moves."

"It *moves?*"

"Well, yeah. That's when I noticed it."

The nurse stood, giving him a strained smile.

"The doctor will be in to see you." She said, handing him a blue and white gown. "Take off your shirt and slip this on. You can keep your pants."

"No foreplay then?" Mark joked, as she turned on her heel and left the room.

"I guess not." He said with a sigh, slipping into the gown and sitting on the exam table with his hands hanging between his knees.

He wasn't afraid of the doctor's office, but wearing the thin linen gown made him feel like a child. Though he'd been healthy most of his childhood, it seemed his entire youth had been spent in rooms like this one. His mother had been a paranoid sort, rushing him in for every sneeze and sniffle.

"Hey Mark, how's it going?" Dr. Alex McDonald didn't knock before entering; they had been friends for many years. He sat on his stool and wheeled over to shake Mark's hand.

"Been better, Alex."

"What's going on with you?" As he spoke, Alex palpated Mark's neck, checking the lymph nodes, then looked in his ears.

"Well, I guess there's a worm in my eye." Mark cringed as he said it.

"A worm in your eye?" Alex laughed, his brow furrowed.

"Yeah. This morning I had a bad pain in my left eye and when I looked in the mirror I saw it. Not much thicker than a thread, but fairly long. It wiggled across the white of my eye, under the surface. Freaked me the fuck out."

"Can you feel it now?" Alex looked concerned, his smile fading. He pulled back Mark's eyelids and peered into the left eye with his ophthalmoscope.

"Not really, but my joints have been aching off and on and I keep getting a rash that fades after a few days. I thought maybe I was getting the flu."

"How long have the other symptoms been present?" Alex scribbled on a notepad, much like the unpleasant nurse.

"Oh, maybe a few months." Mark felt the sting of tears in his eyes, his palms sweating. He knew parasites were a job hazard, could handle the thought of a tape worm or chiggers, but in his eye?

"Okay, Mark. We'll get to the bottom of this. From the looks of your chart, I gave you a malaria shot around three years ago. You were going to Africa, am I right?"

"Yeah. I went to the Congo to photograph a group of western lowland gorillas."

"Yes, yes. I remember that now. Stunning photos, by the way."

"Thank you. Do you think I picked something up in Africa?"

"Possibly. I have an idea what's going on here, but give me minute to do some research. I'll be right back and we'll figure out what to do, bud." Alex patted Mark on the shoulder and disappeared out the door.

Mark waited on the table, nervous. After what seemed like an eternity, the doctor walked back in the room and sat on his stool, his mouth set in a serious line, though his eyes danced with excitement.

"Well Mark, it looks like you've picked up a case of loiasis. Have you heard of it?"

"Sounds vaguely familiar. What is it, in *English please.*"

"What you saw in your eye is a Loa loa worm, otherwise known as an African Eye Worm. You can get it through the bite of an infected mango fly and it may take years to present any symptoms. The worms themselves can live up to seventeen years and cause all kinds of trouble from colonic damage to testicular swelling. We will have to do a blood test to be sure, but I'd bet my eyeteeth that's what it is." Alex laughed when Mark cringed at the term *eyeteeth.* "Sorry, man. I know it's freaky. I would've never guessed I'd actually get to see a case of Loa loa in person."

"Glad I made your day, Doc." Mark said sarcastically. "What do we do now?"

"Well, from what I've read, the best chance of detecting the microfilariae in your blood,"

"*English,* Doc."

"The *baby worms.* Anyway, the best chance we have of detecting them in a blood test would be to wait until around noon tomorrow. That's when they are present in the highest concentration. So you come back at, say twelve-thirty tomorrow and we'll do the tests. Think of it as a lunch date with Loa loa." Alex smiled and Mark grimaced.

"Funny. Okay, so then what?"

"If you test positive, we will get you on some medication to kill the worms."

"Worms?" Mark felt his stomach lurch.

"Oh, yeah. If you have one, there's probably hundreds more."

***

The following afternoon, Mark once again sat waiting in an exam room for Alex. His blood had been drawn and they were awaiting the test results. The doctor finally entered and shook his hand again, before clapping him on the shoulder and taking his seat.

"The tests were positive. Your little buddy is in fact a Loa loa worm." Alex did his best to look grave, but Mark knew he was delighted to add this to his list of unusual cases.

"Okay, so what do we do to get rid of my *little buddy?*"

"There are a few options. We could surgically remove it, but we have to catch it when it's actually crossing the eye, and that's not going to be easy. Also, that would leave the rest of the worms in your system. There are a few drug options, some more effective than others, but they have risks of side effects. Most of the side effects happen in a person who is heavily infested, but the good news is that you are not. I would like to hit this hard with the most powerful drug, DEC. It runs the highest risks of complication, such as encephalopathy and death, but you are strong and healthy, with a relatively mild infestation."

"All right." Mark shuddered, horrified that he had the parasites, no matter how mild the case.

Alex scribbled his prescription on a notepad, then tore off the top sheet and handed it to Mark.

"Take this to the pharmacy. I doubt they have it in stock, but they'll be able to order it. You will take the pills three times a day for the next three weeks."

"Three weeks?" Mark said, dismayed at the thought of living with the Loa loa for three more weeks.

"Mmm-hmm. We will retest your blood then. Only about fifty-percent get by with one round of DEC. There's a chance you might have to go another three weeks on top of that."

"Fantastic." Mark grumbled.

"And Mark, no alcohol at all during this time. A large number of subjects with adverse reactions reported to have consumed alcohol. So *no alcohol*, okay?" Alex fixed him with a stern look.

"Alright, Doc. I've got it. No fun."

***

The Loa loa made its appearance five more times during the first couple of weeks Mark was on the DEC. It always started with a sharp pain in his left eye, coupled with the previously unsettling and now awful feeling of movement under his eyelid. Despite the ache in his eye, he could feel it *sliding* just beneath the surface, inching its way around.

Sometimes it felt like a bubble, wriggling and pushing against the lid. Mark found himself bolting to the bathroom each time to watch its progress. Just under the iris, his sclera would look bubbled, the thread-thin worm starting its trek that took from ten to fifteen minutes. Mark guessed it could be as much as an inch or two in length, but it was hard to tell as the worm wriggled its way across, just beneath the surface membrane of his eyeball.

By the third week, the Loa loa appeared to be dead, and lab tests confirmed that the DEC had removed the larvae from his blood. Mark breathed a sigh of relief and went on with his life. He pointedly avoided looking in the toilet after crapping, afraid he might see what looked like spaghetti in there.

***

One morning, nearly a month later, when the episode with the Loa loa was an unpleasant but fading memory, Mark awoke with a crushing headache. It felt as though someone was pounding the right side of his head with a hammer. Dizzy and disoriented, he got out of bed and staggered to the bathroom to retrieve some aspirin from the medicine cabinet, took four, and collapsed on the couch. At least it was Sunday, and he could stay in his apartment and watch football.

By the afternoon, the headache hadn't subsided and, even worse, Mark noticed a change in his vision.

I wonder if this is what a migraine feels like, he thought, returning to the bathroom for more aspirin.

He studied his haggard reflection in the mirror. Something was wrong. Leaning in close to examine his eyes, he gasped and took a step back.

"What the fuck?"

Mark looked at his eyes again and shook his head in bewilderment. His right eye was still the familiar pale blue, but his left pupil was now ringed in brown. Squeezing his eyes shut for a second before opening them again, Mark felt a sharp pain shoot through the right side of his head. He gripped the sink for support, his vision blurred.

After the world stopped spinning, he looked in the mirror again and closed just his left eye. His vision cleared and the dizziness retreated. He closed the right eye, leaving the left open and his stomach lurched.

Darkness.

Mark was blind in his left eye.

***

"I don't know what to tell you, Mr. Hanks." The ophthalmologist sat back and scratched his chin. "From all my testing, it seems your eye is working just fine. It reacts the way it should to light and other stimuli. I have no idea why you can't see through it."

Mark had called Alex right away, but was told his problem was beyond the scope of his practice and was immediately referred to an eye doctor. Now the eye doctor was telling him there was nothing wrong with his eye.

"What about the color change? What would cause that?" Mark turned his useless left eye away from the doctor so he could see him better through his right.

"That's strange. I have heard of brown-eyed patients suddenly turning blue, but that is an anomaly that only occurs in centurions and no one really knows what causes it. But blue eyes turning brown? Not after two years of age or so."

"Is there anything we can do?" Knowing he had been harboring a worm in his eye was bad, but it was nothing compared to the fear of going blind. Mark panicked, thinking of how many changes this would cause in his life, one of them being the end of his career as a photographer. "Is my other eye at risk?"

"It's hard to say, but I doubt it. I've never seen anything like this, but if I had to hazard a guess, maybe the Loa loa did some damage in your left eye that I can't detect. Short of having your regular doctor order an MRI, I don't know how to proceed further here."

"I'll call Dr. Alex and ask for an MRI. I *need* my eyes." Mark was frustrated by the ophthalmologist's perplexed attitude.

"Okay, tell him I would appreciate it if he would send the copy of the report to my office right away."

Mark walked out the door, the bright afternoon sunlight

stinging his freshly dilated right eye, forcing him to put on his sunglasses. As he slipped into the driver's seat, his glasses slid down his nose and he caught sight of his eyes in the rearview mirror. Despite the blurriness in his good eye, he could see instantly there had been a change. No longer just ringed in darkness, his left eye was now completely brown.

***

Mark was in the toiletry aisle of the grocery store the first time the voice spoke to him. It was so clear and close that he stopped immediately and looked around. He was alone.

Minutes later, at the meat counter, it spoke again.

"Nipe msaada!" *I need help!*

Looking around again, Mark caught the eye of a man waiting at the other end of the meat case.

"Excuse me." Mark smiled at the portly man, who returned the smile hesitantly. "Did you just hear someone speaking Swahili?"

The other man shook his head, then looked at his watch and mumbled something about being late before hurrying away.

The voice spoke to him for the third time as he sat at his kitchen table, eating a meal of beef stew and French bread.

After a thorough search of his apartment, including closets and under the bed, Mark came to the unsettling conclusion that the voice was coming from his own head.

Mark sat on his couch with the television on, but couldn't pay attention to the show. That foreign voice in his head kept jabbering, sometimes laughing and other times sounding angry and harsh. His pulse raced as he fought to quell his rising panic.

What the fuck is going on with me?

Unbidden memories of his mother raced through his head. His mother worrying over a random fever, wringing her hands so hard her knuckles cracked. Her harassing phone calls whenever he went to a friend's house, certain the other parents could never take care of him as she could. Then the time he found her in the shower, curled into a fetal position and shrieking. The paramedics took her away in restraints as she wailed for her son.

She ended up killing herself with one bullet to the roof of her mouth after leaving a hastily scrawled note of apology to her only child.

"No." Mark said to the empty room, then again with more force. "No!"

He was not going crazy. He had worked too hard to get where he was in life to let it be ruined by some inherited insanity. He would ignore it. He would *will* the voice away. He could do this.

Mark went into the kitchen and pulled out a rocks glass, filling it with ice. A bottle of bourbon sat on the counter, untouched since he'd started taking medicine for the Loa loa worm. He poured the amber fluid into the glass, his nervousness causing him to spill a bit on the counter. Not bothering to wipe it up, he started back to the living room, then returned for the rest of the bottle.

The bourbon burned down his throat, but he liked the feeling. When the glass was empty, he made to fill it again but changed his mind, swigging directly from the bottle. He felt the warmth of a pleasant buzz as the voice seemed to quiet down a bit, its interjection coming less and less.

Mark kept drinking.

Hours later, just before he passed out on the couch, Mark heard the voice speak one more time. He couldn't help but laugh as the phantom in his head slurred in Swahili.

***

The MRI hummed and clicked around him, but Mark lay on the table unfazed, drifting in and out of consciousness from the sedatives the nurse had given him. He'd learned years ago, after a failed MRI for a torn rotator cuff, that he was claustrophobic and needed sedation to remain still for the forty-five minute procedure.

Drifting into sleep, Mark found himself in the jungles of the Congo once again, his guide speaking softly in accented English. The man's pleasant face swam in and out of focus, but he could hear him warning of the dangers of the jungle.

"The gorillas aren't the only things to fear in the jungle, Sir. It's a haunted place, full of many bad spirits. You be careful one doesn't hop inside you."

A mango fly bit his leg and Mark watched it drink his blood, knowing he should slap it away, but unable to move.

"Stop." He giggled drunkenly. "You'll give me the Loa loa."

Something crashed to his right, unseen in the deep darkness of the inner jungle and he was afraid. The gorillas. He had to be careful not to anger them. They could be lethal. The foliage parted and something huge and pale reared up before Mark. Not a gorilla, but a Loa loa worm, freakishly large and bearing down on him with an open mouth full of razor sharp teeth.

Mark awoke with a cry.

"It's all right, Mr. Hanks. The testing is done."

He was laying on the table, his arms held down by his sides with heavy blankets and his head wedged into place by foam cushions on each side. A nurse removed the folded washcloth from his eyes, and he blinked at the sudden brightness of the overhead fluorescents.

"Oh my God." Mark said to the nurse, his right eye opened wide in alarm, his left still half-lidded from sedation.

"What is it, Mr. Hanks? Are you going to be ill?" The nurse looked concerned, placing a gentle hand on his brow.

"I *know*. I know what it is!" Mark tried to sit up, but a wave of dizziness overcame him. He needed to throw up, barely making it into the wastebasket the nurse held before his face. When he was finished, he wiped his mouth with a towel, his shoulders slumped.

"Are you okay?" The nurse asked.

"I don't know. But I know what it is now. I need to talk to Alex." Mark felt cold sweat trickle down his sides, tickling across his ribcage. He tried to stand, but the nurse put a restraining hand on his shoulder.

"I don't think you should stand just yet, Mr. Hanks. Let's give the sedatives a chance to wear off." She pulled up a stool and sat in front of him, patting him reassuringly on the knee. It felt like a weird gesture to Mark, not something a stranger would do. His mind spun with the knowledge his dream had uncovered.

"I have to talk to Alex." He said, then vomited again.

***

"I'm not crazy, Alex." Mark leaned across the table, his eyes boring into his friend's.

"Not saying you are, bud. It's just a precaution." Alex sipped his beer and shrugged. "Given your Mom's history."

"She was schizophrenic. I'm not schizophrenic. When have you ever known me to be anything other than on an even keel? Have I ever done anything crazy around you? I mean, Christ Alex, we've been friends for years. You of all people should know I'm not insane."

"I know, Mark. The MRI was clear, but maybe that worm did something we can't see. Changed your brain chemistry, or something. I just think it wouldn't hurt to talk to a psychiatrist. If there's damage we can't see, maybe he can prescribe something to make your hallucinations go away. Hell, he might be able to get you the sight back in your eye if the cause is psychiatric. Please. Just go see him. Dr. Whitehead is the best. It's a place to start until we can figure out where to turn next."

Mark sat back and closed his right eye, but the left stayed open of its own accord and looked around.

"I don't know." He rubbed his temples.

"Come on. It can't hurt anything. If nothing else, it will prove you're not schizophrenic. And you can't tell me it's not digging away at the back of your mind that it's hereditary." Alex smiled, but his eyes remained concerned. "Just do it for me. If Dr. Whitehead can't help you, I *promise* I will hook you up with whatever specialists you need."

Mark finished his beer and grimaced as the voice yelled its foreign gibberish in his head.

"All right. Schedule the appointment."

***

Dr. Emmanuel Whitehead was a pleasant looking man, with just a trace of a foreign accent that lent a certain trustworthiness to his words. He appeared to be anywhere from fifty to seventy, with grey hair, slightly stooped shoulders, and compassionate blue eyes.

Under different circumstances, Mark would've enjoyed the man's company; but given what his appointment was for, he felt anxious and skeptical instead. Dr. Whitehead had him sit in an overstuffed armchair identical to the one the doctor sat in. Mark recognized the tactic, making him feel as though they were equals. He wondered if it worked on crazy people.

"So tell me what you think is going on with you, Mark." Dr. Whitehead smiled and glanced at a notebook on his lap. He began to scratch down notes before Mark even spoke.

"Well, I know that the Loa loa is gone, and the eye doctor can't explain the change in my left eye—"

"The change?" The doctor raised a brow.

"Yeah, my eye changed from blue to brown and I lost the sight in it, though the eye doctor said everything seems to work in there."

"Blue to brown? It hasn't always been that way? Fascinating. What did he suppose happened there?"

"I told you he doesn't know. *Anyway,* there's nothing on the MRI and I've started hearing a voice in my head." Mark glanced up from his hands, trying to gauge the doctor's reaction, but the man simply regarded him without expression. "The voice seems to be speaking Swahili."

"How do you know it's Swahili? Do you speak Swahili?" Dr. Whitehead's brow furrowed a bit.

"No, I don't. But I spent some time in the Congo a few years back. I'm a photographer and I had an assignment to photograph the gorillas. My guide spoke English, but a lot of the people I encountered didn't. The voice sounds like they did, and I recognize a few words."

"So you don't know for a fact that it's Swahili."

"No. I guess not." Mark frowned, unsure where this was going.

"Would it be safe to say that the voice may not be speaking a language at all? That it could be gibberish?"

"No. It's not gibberish. I don't understand what he's saying, but I know it's a language and it sounds like Swahili. He said *I need help,* at one point."

"He?" The doctor tilted his head, looking quizzical.

"What?"

"You just said *he.* Up until now, you have referred to the voice as *it.*"

"What the hell does *that* matter? So I said he. The voice sounds male, deep like a man's. I mean who gives a fuck?" Mark stood and began to pace the floor. "I told Alex this was a mistake."

"Please, Mark. I'm just trying to help you." Dr. Whitehead's placating tone made Mark want to punch the man in his pleasant face.

"That's better." The doctor said as Mark reluctantly returned to his seat. "Do you have an idea as to the identity of this speaker in your mind?"

"Yeah." The anger ran out of Mark in a rush and he wilted in the chair. "It came to me in a dream during the MRI."

"A dream?"

"If you keep repeating everything I say, I swear I'm out the door."

"I'm sorry, Mark. I will try to refrain. You were telling me about your dream."

"No I wasn't. I don't want to talk about the dream."

"We can't get to the bottom of this if we don't discuss it, Mark."

"Discuss it? You just repeat everything I say and scribble in your goddamn notebook! And you keep saying my name to make me feel like we're buddies, but I doubt you're even paying attention to me." Mark glanced at his watch. "The hour is almost up, anyway."

Dr. Whitehead set the notebook and pen on the table between them before leaning forward in his seat and folding his hands between his knees. He stared unflinchingly at Mark with his soft eyes and smiled.

"I'm listening, Mark. I mean, I'm listening. Please tell me about the dream. You have my undivided attention."

"No. There's no time left. I'll tell you what I think, though."
Mark stood. "I don't know how it happened, and I don't know
why, but somehow one of those jungle spirits got into my head.
Maybe he hitched a ride on the Loa loa and took up shop in my
brain when the thing died, but he's there. And he's taken over
my left eye. That's why it turned brown and I can't see out of it.
Sure it still works. But it's working for *him.* And I need to stop
this before he takes over something else."

Dr. Whitehead said nothing at first, just sat there and looked
thoughtful, as if he was honestly considering the possibility of
Mark's story. He then picked up the notebook and flipped back a
few pages, squinting at his own illegible writing as he reviewed
something in silence. When he looked at Mark again, his face
looked both grave and sympathetic.

"Mark, it says here that your mother was diagnosed
schizophrenic—"

"Fuck you."

***

Mark sat at the kitchen table with a makeup mirror
purchased from a secondhand store propped up before him. He
could hear the water on the stove boiling, signaling it was almost
time. He waited, just the sound of the water and the prattle of
his Swahili ghost to keep him company. It had been almost a
week since he had stormed out of Dr. Whitehead's office, and Alex
had called him no less than thirty times before Mark finally told
him to stop.

Someone pounded on the door and Mark got up to peek
through the peephole. It was Alex, his face distorted by the lens.

"What do you want, Alex?" He yelled through the door.

"Let me in, Mark. I want to talk to you. I'm worried about you."

"Nope. Go away. I don't have anything to say to you."

"Goddamnit, Mark! Open up or I'm calling the cops!" Alex's
voice broke at the end, and Mark thought he might be close to
tears.

"No good, old friend. There's no law against refusing to leave
your house. But there is one against trespassing." Mark walked

back to the table and sat down. When his cell phone rang, he shut it off without looking, certain it was Alex again. The fucker had been talking to Dr. Whitehead. He wasn't a friend of *Mark's* anymore.

Almost time, Mark thought, leaning in close to the mirror. *Better test this out first.* He raised his finger toward his left eye. It snapped shut, protecting itself from the questing digit. He heard the foreign voice in his head complain, but he ignored it. Prying the lid open with the thumb and forefinger of his left hand, Mark pressed on the eyeball with his right index finger, causing the voice to shriek in pain.

Just as I thought. I can't feel a thing.

Mark stood and wandered into the kitchen to collect his tools. A bottle of rubbing alcohol awaited him on the counter and the pot still bubbled away on the stove. Turning off the burner, he used a pair of tongs to retrieve a long thin blade from the boiling water and set it on the counter. Finding a pot holder in the drawer, he carefully wrapped it around the handle of the knife and grabbed the alcohol in his other hand, then returned to his seat.

Mark hadn't enjoyed a moment's peace in almost a week. All day and night the voice babbled, disappearing just long enough for him to fall asleep, only to wake him moments later with mocking laughter. It was a game for the spirit, one Mark was losing. He stopped eating altogether and only drank whisky, hoping to get the ghost drunk enough that it would allow him to rest. But nothing worked. Mark knew if he didn't do something soon, he would die of hunger and exhaustion, leaving his body vacant for the spirit to completely take over. He refused to let that happen.

Transferring the wrapped blade carefully to his left hand, he squeezed the bottle of alcohol between his thighs, unscrewing the cap with his right. The alcohol made a hissing sound when he poured it over the knife, giving off a cloud of astringent steam that burned his good eye. Before he could lose his nerve or allow the knife to cool anymore, he touched the tip of the blade to his left cheek, just under the eye and pushed. It was amazing how easily the blade cut through the flesh of the lid, spearing the eyeball beneath with a pop. The voice in his head gibbered its agony, wailing in a language he didn't understand, but conveying a terror that satisfied Mark.

"Take that, you bastard!" Mark twisted the knife in the socket, his stomach churning as thick jelly and dark blood welled from the wound, running down his face in a viscous rivulet. He felt nothing but triumph as he kept cutting, slicing away at his eyelids, carving out a raw, red hole in his skull. There wasn't as much blood as he had expected, the hot blade cauterized most of the blood vessels, but soon the knife cooled and he no longer smelled the scorched tissues.

Mark threw the knife back into the pot and returned it to a boil.

Not done yet.

He didn't have to understand the language to know the spirit was alternately pleading with him and cursing him. He felt no sympathy as he waited for the knife to heat again. He was going to get rid of it even if he killed himself in the process.

Mark regarded his face in the mirror, too tired to feel any real shock as he looked at the ragged red hole where his left eye used to be. Thick fluids still oozed down his face, and he did nothing to clean them off.

You look like shit, old boy! he thought, unable to stop the manic giggle that bubbled up from his chest. *Almost done here. Then some rest.*

With the hot blade back in his right hand, he probed the empty socket with the tip, trying to determine the best angle for his task. Bracing himself for the force that would be required to breach his skull, Mark halted at the last second, adrenaline making his heart pound in his chest like a tribal drum.

"Oh shit! Oh shit! I almost fucked up bad there." He said to the voice in his head, which had gone eerily quiet. "You would've liked that wouldn't you? You wanted me to make that mistake. Fuck you, though. I aced anatomy."

Pulling the tip of the knife out of his ruined eye socket, Mark winced when the blade touched the flesh beneath his right eye. This was going to hurt like hell, but it didn't matter. He could take it. He could take anything to quiet that voice. He had come close to fucking it all up, but had remembered just in time. That's right, one Anatomy class fifteen years ago had saved him from disaster. He smiled as he pressed down, ignoring the flaring pain. The left eye is controlled by the *right* brain.

***

"This next case is an unfortunate one of Schizophrenia left undiagnosed." Dr. Whitehead led a small group of residents down the hall, telling them the details of the patient in each room. As they walked, the men and women scribbled furiously in their notepads, trying to cram in every word the well-known psychiatrist said. "Jonathan, if you would."

A large orderly stepped forward, produced a ring of keys from his pocket, and unlocked the door. They all took turns peeking into the room, their manners silent and respectful, though one young woman winced when she saw the man.

"Is that self-mutilation?" the lady asked.

"Yes." Dr. Whitehead nodded. He looked in, seeing the patient had once again removed the dressings from his face, exposing dark, gaping eye sockets and the scarred flesh around them. The patient turned his face toward the sound of the doctor's voice and smiled, his head lolling slightly from medication.

"His delusions caused him to believe that a ghost had taken up residence in his head. I only had the preliminary visit with him before a neighbor reported screaming from his apartment and called the authorities. By the time the door came down, the patient had already removed both his eyes and pushed a hot knife into the right side of his brain."

"Fascinating. He's lucky to be alive," a male student remarked.

"Yes. But there have been a great many people who have survived with only half of their brains. Then again, most of those cases have involved surgery of a more orthodox form than this one." Dr. Whitehead smiled and the students chuckled politely.

"Does he still hold the delusions that a ghost resides in his head." The same woman as before spoke, looking up expectantly from her notes.

"That's hard to tell. Since he regained consciousness, the patient acts as though he can't understand English."

As if to prove the point, the patient spoke. "Nipe Msaada."

"Gibberish?"

"Actually no." Dr. Whitehead frowned a bit, nodding to Jonathan and watching as the orderly relocked the door before answering. At the sound of the lock turning, the patient began to yell and Dr. Whitehead listened for a moment to the cadence of the speech before speaking. "This patient is speaking Swahili."

INK

"**I**T'S NOT FAIR."

Andrea spoke a little too loudly, attracting glances from nearby diners. "My brother is dead and they get away scotch free!"

"*Scot-free,*" Stella corrected softly.

"What?"

"It's scot-free. Not scotch free."

"Who cares?" She waved a well-manicured hand. "I can't believe the judge didn't hold them responsible for Michael's death."

Stella pinched the bridge of her nose with her thumb and forefinger, trying in vain to stave off the headache that always seemed to come when she spent any amount of time with her young sister-in-law.

"It was an accident, Andrea. Suing the restaurant isn't going to bring him back."

"Maybe not, but it's not fair. Someone should be punished for this. Someone screwed up and I lost my brother. And it wasn't an accident. Noel said that someone was directly responsible. It was murder."

"Who said it was murder?" Stella kept her own voice low, hoping Andrea might follow suit.

"Noel. You know, my psychic. From the psychic advisor forum. I know I've mentioned her about a hundred times. Don't you *ever* listen?" Andrea rolled her eyes.

"Yeah. The psychic. Sorry. So you're doing all of this because some woman you met online says she knows that someone murdered Michael." The urge to wring Andrea's slim neck–grew every time the girl opened her mouth. "How much are you paying this woman?"

"Enough. Don't worry about it. She's worth every penny. Noel said that Michael was murdered. That's good enough for me. It never really felt like an accident, anyway. Not really. Deep in my heart it always felt like murder. I can't believe you aren't more supportive of this. He was your *husband* after all."

"Damnit Andrea, it's been over a year. You think you're the only one who misses him? At least you still have Rick and the kids. I have nobody anymore. Just the house. I still have to sleep in that big bed alone, knowing that Michael will never be snoring next to me again. Hell, I even miss the snoring." Stella dabbed at the corners of her eyes with a linen napkin before her mascara could start to run. "He was my whole world, but I accept that he is gone and nothing I could ever do would bring him back. It's about time that you accept it, too."

Andrea reached across the table and patted Stella's hand, her face full of remorse.

She was silly and selfish at times, and extremely stubborn, but she wasn't a deliberately cruel person. A lifetime of wealth and being pampered by her parents, then by her older brother after their folks were killed in a car accident, had left Andrea with little idea of how things worked in the real world. She was the only link Stella still had to Michael.

"I'm sorry, Stella. I know you've suffered, too. And you're not alone. You are a part of our family, too. Rick and the kids adore you, and you're like a sister to me. That's why I'm doing this for the both of us. No matter what you say, I know we will both sleep better once there's justice for Michael, once the killer pays for taking him from us."

"What are you talking about? The judge ruled it an accident. The case is closed." Stella would've given anything to be home in bed right then, rather than sitting in a fancy restaurant listening to Andrea's schemes, but their weekly lunch dates were a tradition her sister-in-law had insisted should continue on.

At first Stella had thought Andrea was doing it for her, to keep her in some sort of routine, but quickly realized the lunches were also Andrea's much needed diversion from the daily demands of motherhood.

The waiter interrupted then, bringing them the bill for their sandwiches and wine.

Andrea snatched it off the table and produced a platinum card from her small purse with a flourish. She didn't speak again until after the waiter returned with the receipt, leaving with her signature and a healthy tip.

"It's not over yet." Finally, she dropped her voice low, leaning over the table toward Stella, her eyes alight with a cold sparkle.

"What do you mean?" Stella felt herself leaning in as well, against her volition.

"Noel introduced me to someone. A guy that handles these sorts of things, though I'm not allowed to speak his name out loud. He's going to take care of it for me." Andrea smiled, though it was a hard expression, with little mirth.

"You're going to have to be a little more specific, dear." Stella frowned. "Because I'm not following. How does he *take care* of these things?"

"I'm not sure how it works exactly. Witchcraft, voodoo, hoodoo. All I know is that he has magic. And he promised to make the murderer pay. Like a curse or something."

Andrea looked so serious.

Stella instantly regretted the laugh that escaped her, knowing the outrage and hurt on the other woman's face was her fault. Despite the damage to Andrea's ego, a few more giggles slipped out before a sobering thought occurred to her, erasing the hilarity of the situation instantly.

"Oh God, Andrea! Please tell me you haven't been meeting with these people."

"Of course not. I'm not stupid. The whole transaction took place online." Andrea sniffed, her eyes squinted in offense like she smelled something bad and just realized Stella was the source.

"Transaction? You mean you paid this guy?"

"Of course I paid him. He wasn't going to do it for free."

"With a credit card? Oh Christ! These people will clean you out. What if they're scam artists, Andrea? How could you be so dumb?" Stella regretted the words the moment she spoke, but the damage was already done.

"I won't talk about this anymore," Andrea said, her jaw tight and her eyes downcast. "I think I should take you home."

"Yeah. I think that's a good idea."

***

The drive to her house was long and filled with a tense silence while Stella tried a hundred times to form the right words to apologize. In the end, she just blurted it out, not willing to open the car door until things were better between them.

"Look, I'm sorry Andrea. I didn't mean it the way it came out. You know I love you and I worry, right? It's okay if you want to believe in that stuff, but when they start taking your money, well, I get defensive of you. I want closure as badly as you do, sweetie. But I don't think paying some guy to get revenge for an accident is the way."

Andrea nodded, reaching over to hug her sister-in-law. After the awkward embrace, Stella smiled and pulled away.

"How about we go shoe shopping tomorrow? It's been a while since I got a new pair of shoes."

"Yeah. We could do that." Andrea sniffed a bit, but smiled softly. "I'll come by tomorrow to get you. Noon? We could do lunch again."

"Sounds great." Stella got out of the car and stood in the

driveway, waving as Andrea backed out onto the road. When her sister-in-law was gone from sight, she turned back to the house and just stood, staring at it. Her dream house.

She remembered how excited she had been when they first saw it. How her heart had hammered in her chest, and how she refused to look at any other places, begging Michael until he bid on this one. How she made him raise the amount twice when they learned others had shown serious interest. It was still beautiful. It was still everything she had ever wanted in a home, but lately it felt like just a house.

Walking in through the front door, she averted her eyes from the couch by the picture window, but still saw it in her mind. The cop on his knees, retrieving Michael's Epi-pen from underneath the sofa, not in the breast pocket of his jacket where it belonged. Stella hadn't sat on that couch for over a year now. Every time she tried, she saw the sad look on the cop's face, the apologetic shake of his head. His soft words to the grieving widow.

"It wasn't your fault, ma'am. It must've fallen out and rolled under."

Stella walked through the dining room to the fridge, retrieving a chilled bottle of Moscato and a wine glass from the cupboard. A sweet wine with a dry and bitter aftertaste, like a marriage could be.

Leaning against the counter, she stared at the empty dinette table where they had eaten their last meal, trying hard not to see the panic on his face as he realized some incompetent cook had allowed a single piece of shrimp to contaminate his take-out chicken stir-fry. After a few seconds she closed her eyes, letting the images come, knowing they would prick at her senses until she gave in.

She saw his handsome face turning red, his smooth voice gasping for her to retrieve the rescue syringe, hands digging at the outside of his throat as if this could somehow stop the swelling within. Those hands reaching for her from where he had fallen to the floor when she returned empty handed, his face purple, his eyes bulging and begging for help. She heard her own tearful plea for help from the operator, and the whine of the ambulance in the driveway.

The whoosh of breath from the paramedic performing CPR as he dropped his weight on her husband's chest, his clenched hands breaking Michael's ribs. The soft beeping sound of the machines in the hospital, slowing then stopping as they unplugged the life support and let him go. The sound of Andrea wailing that *they couldn't be sure, he might not be brain dead!*

Stella wiped her tears with the back of her hand and finished her wine in one long gulp, before refilling the glass once again. She toasted the empty chair at the head of the table.

"I miss you, Michael. I never knew I could miss you this much."

The two glasses of Moscato on top of the martinis she drank at lunch, along with the recent onslaught of melancholic memories began to conspire against her. Stella placed her glass gently in the sink before stumbling to the bedroom. Collapsing upon the bed she and Michael had shared for five years, she gave in to the sobs and cried herself to sleep.

***

Stella woke from a nightmare so awful her stomach churned, sending her scrambling to the bathroom in just enough time to see the day's meal and alcohol reappear into the toilet. When her retching had subsided, she turned the shower on as hot as she could stand it, and stood beneath the scalding stream, the remnants of the dream fading slowly. She knew that in it Michael had been alive again. She could hear the fading echoes of his voice calling her vain. Calling her a whore.

Standing before the full length mirror she ran her hands gently across her bare body, stopping to caress the concave smoothness of her belly before trailing her fingertips over the small tattoo on her right hip. Michael had hated it, saying it looked trashy and marred her otherwise perfect body, but Stella loved that tiny rosebud with its delicate, encircling thorny vine. Leaning her forehead against the cool mirror, she let her hand wander back to her stomach with a heavy sigh and thought about what was really behind the nightmare. The fight. That stupid, wretched fight.

In five years of marriage, Michael and Stella had their share of quarrels like any other couple, but that last one had been different. There had been such a hardness in Michael when he said he would leave her. She'd known he meant it. She couldn't even blame him for it. Not really. Hadn't she been the one to lead him on about his desires for a family, only to find every excuse possible to put it off?

She'd been the one lying to him, saying they would try for a baby while secretly taking the pill for years. She'd even let him go to the doctor and get tested, when he believed their failure to conceive had been because of him. It was only natural he would feel betrayed upon finding her birth control, tucked deep in the cabinet behind her tampons where she thought for certain he would never look.

It was even her fault that he had come to the conclusion he had about *why* she did it. She hadn't corrected him when he said she was vain and didn't want to ruin her body with a child. That she was selfish and didn't want to be saddled with the care of another human being's needs. It was even almost true.

If only Stella had been honest with Michael. She could've shared her deepest fears with him. He was her husband, the one person with whom she was supposed to hold back nothing. She knew in her heart he would've forgiven her. He would've maybe reassured her, and she could've left all those fears behind. Michael had loved her. Despite whatever failings he may have had, he always loved her.

Stella stepped back and looked at her reflection again, cupping first one small breast, then the other and releasing them, observing for any sign of sagging. Maybe she should get that boob job Michael had refused to let her have. Her breasts still looked good, but they could stand to be a bit bigger.

What Michael hadn't known was, at the root of her vanity lay fear. The terror of being thrust back into poverty, to struggle for everything she ever had, like she did before she married Michael.

He had never been poor. Never known what it was like to have nothing but your looks to get you by. Never had to use his looks to fight his way through the world.

What if she had a few kids and Michael stopped loving her? What if her stretch marks and sagging tits made her so unappealing that he started having affairs? What if he left her for a younger woman? It happened every day. Men almost routinely left the women who had borne and raised their children for younger, more attractive girls. What would she have then? In the end, it was a risk she hadn't been able to take, and when Michael found out, he had been devastated. Though she'd calmed him and promised to work it out, she knew that he would've left her soon. The rift was too much to repair.

Leaving her robe on the hook behind the door, Stella walked through the house, stepping out onto the back porch where floodlights reflected off the swimming pool's blue water. The ocean's surf crashed a few blocks away, another thing Michael had taken exception to. She could hear him in her head: *Having a swimming pool this close to the ocean is pretentious, dear. We will look like assholes.* Stella didn't care. Deep down, she *liked* pretentious. She *deserved* pretentious. The high fence around the backyard prevented all but those in the upper levels of the neighboring houses from seeing her nudity, though their windows were dark.

The night was warm, but the water made her gasp when she entered, each step submerging more of her, until the cold slipped over her breasts in a pleasant sensation that took her breath away and chased off any lingering, brooding thoughts. Stella swam laps until her limbs felt rubbery with exhaustion, then reclined on the steps, allowing her body to float out in front of her as she rested her buoyant weight on her elbows. She wondered what it would be like to just let the water soothe her to sleep, slipping under to drown in her slumber. Something splashed into the far end of the pool, a soft noise she heard but disregarded without opening her eyes.

The floodlights flickered, then went out, leaving Stella to float in the dark. Her heart lurched and began to pound with fear. *Don't be a ninny, it's just a rolling blackout. Too many people in the city running their air conditioners.* She laughed to herself, but the sound did little to calm her nerves. With the moon behind a cloud, the night was pitch black, and the sound of the surf seemed to swell in the darkness. She reached out a hand and could barely see it before her face. *Time to get out.*

As Stella sat up on the steps, a strange sensation made her pause. A tickling started at her hip, before slowly spreading up her side to her breast, as if someone were lightly running their fingertip across her bare flesh. Goosebumps rose along her body as a wave of heat followed the path to her nipple, pleasure exploding from its peak to wash over her.

She laid back slightly, the pleasant feeling causing her to moan. There had been no one since Michael's death, no lovers beside her own infrequent masturbation, and the unexpected rush paralyzed her with pleasure. It spread to the other breast and she nearly cried out from the intensity. Twin lovers suckled her breasts, though no one shared the pool with her and her hands floated by her sides. The tickling wove from her hip around her thigh, where it traced its way across her clit and into her vagina. She gasped and let her thighs fall open, arching her back and thrusting her pelvis upward as the first ripples of orgasm flowed through her body.

Her breasts throbbing with pleasure and her pelvis awash in ecstasy as wave after wave of climax rocked her body, Stella whimpered, all thoughts of the darkness and leaving the pool lost in a haze of sexual splendor. The lights came back on, but she didn't notice, shuddering in the water as her phantom lover worked his magic on her senses, making her cry out her joy. The sensations battered her until she feared she may lose consciousness, drowning in her own pool to be found blue and lifeless in the morning when Andrea came for their shopping spree.

Reluctantly opening her eyes, bewildered by the power of her arousal, Stella glanced down at her body where it floated in the water, and a scream bubbled out of her throat. Something small and strange had attached itself to her tattoo, a jelly-fish like creature with short tentacles and a translucent body. She flicked at it with her hand, but it clung to the flesh, unwilling to be dislodged.

With a cry that was part terror and part revulsion, she squeezed its soft body, gagging as it let go with the sound of a suction cup peeled off glass. She threw it over the edge of the pool, her eyes wide in shock as she looked at what the awful parasite had done to her body. Her legs numb as orgasms continued to rip through her, she crawled up the steps and got to her feet, making her way unsteadily into the house and to the bedroom. Standing before the mirror, hands braced against the wall, her legs threatened to give out as yet another climax rocked her body. Her breasts still throbbed with sensation, though it now bordered on pain.

Stella began to cry as she gazed at her reflection in disbelief. She took one hand off the wall and ran it over her flesh, sobbing as she traced the lines of the tattoo.

Thorny vines that had once encircled the small rose bud on her hip, now streaked up her torso, encircling both her breasts and darkening her nipples. Her torso resembled a demented puzzle, thorny lines covering it in crazy jags. The vines also trailed over hip and across the shaven mound of her sex, disappearing in the cleft.

She bent her knees slightly and spread the fleshy lips apart, crying out when she saw the tattooed vines disappearing into her vagina. Her slick flesh visibly rippled with the force of the pleasure/pain that gripped her pelvis. *No, no, no. It can't be! What the hell is going on? This can't be happening to me!*

Movement on her chest caught Stella's attention, and she looked up at her reflection, her eyes wide in her pale face as she watched the vines grow, dark ink sliding under the skin, across her chest and up to her neck. *Crazy. I'm going crazy!* Large buds began to form on either side of her throat. Her legs gave out as orgasms continued to shake her, now more painful than pleasant. Dropping to her knees, she pressed her forehead against the cool glass of the mirror, watching as the buds continued to grow, starting to bloom on her skin.

An unwanted vision rose in her head. *Andrea finds her dead on the bathroom floor and shakes her head, a voodoo priest replete with painted skull face and feather bedecked staff stands beside her and points at Stella's lifeless form accusingly.*

The buds bloomed fully, revealing a pair of hands that wrapped around Stella's throat, the ink moving fluidly as it spread under her skin. Her face turned red, then purple as she began to cough, no longer able to draw breath as she felt pressure on her windpipe. She could see small blood vessels rupture in her face, dark blotches appearing in spider web patterns. Sliding down the glass, she fell to the floor, her face pressed against her own reflection.

Her own face faded from view, replaced by a ghostly reflection of Michael in the mirror, his face purple with death, but his eyes boring into her own, accusing, *knowing.*

Though there was no way he could've seen into the living room from where he had collapsed onto the floor that night, Stella knew that he knew exactly what happened. And he knew why. Looking into those hate-filled orbs, she saw herself rushing from the kitchen and finding his coat slung over the chair. Grabbing the Epi-pen from the pocket, she watched herself freeze, a look of panicked consideration on her face. She knows what was going through her own mind at the moment. *He's going to divorce me. He will leave me with nothing.*

Stella stands for a moment with the rescue syringe gripped in her hand, then she throws it under the couch, tears streaming down her face as she walks back to the kitchen. Michael reaches a clawed hand toward her, his mouth moving, but no sound emerges. She can read his lips. He says, 'Please.' Grabbing the phone off the cradle, she waits another five minutes after Michael has ceased moving to dial 911. She sobs into the phone asking for help and really wanting it, wanting someone to undo what she has allowed to happen, but it's too late. The events can't be undone.

Stella lay on the floor, unable to breathe as the blood pounded in her head and her chest burned with the effort to draw in air. Her face was pressed against the mirror, but she could no longer see herself or Michael as bright flashes of light overtook her vision. She heard a roar in her ears and a cracking sound as the cartilage of her windpipe gave way. *I take it back. I didn't mean it. I was afraid. I'm so sorry! I take it back!* Darkness took her sight as she drifted into unconsciousness, a searing pain in her chest as her heart sputtered and stilled.

I'm sorry.

BONE PHONE

"**G**ODDAMNIT!" EMILY TRIPPED OVER the box on her way out the front door of her duplex. Hot coffee sloshed over her hand, causing her to drop the mug. It didn't shatter, but the remaining liquid spilled out, soaking the package that had caused all the trouble.

Picking up the coffee mug and placing it on the glass-topped patio table alongside her cigarettes and ashtray, Emily turned back and got the box from where it sat. She carried it over to the table and set it down. She shook a menthol out of the pack and lit it. Taking a deep drag and holding it, she closed her eyes to relish the first cigarette of the morning. With a sigh, she turned her attention back to the package.

The bottom wasn't too wet from the coffee, and it didn't really seem to matter all that much, since the box wasn't in the best shape to begin with. Stained and torn, its construction appeared to be more masking tape than actual cardboard. Nearly illegible, a name and address was scrawled in the lower right hand corner in black marker, but nothing else. No return address. No post marks.

Emily pulled her reading glasses off the top of her head where they were perched more often than not, and squinted to make out the writing.

Dominik Bettancourt. The address was in the city, somewhere downtown.

So how the hell did it wind up out here in the 'burbs? she wondered. Her house was at least an hour and a half drive from downtown, and that was if the traffic was light. Emily shook her head and took another drag of her cigarette.

Lifting the box again, she tested its weight in her hands. Slightly larger than a shoebox, it was fairly heavy, and something inside rattled when she shook it. A frown creased her brow.

Can't exactly open it. It's not mine.

"Good morning."

Emily nearly dropped the box as she spun around to find the postman standing at the bottom of the steps. He smiled and held out a wad of letters for her.

"Um, yeah. Thanks. Say, maybe you could help me with something." She held out the box to him, tipping it forward so he could read the top. "I found this on my porch this morning. I don't know what to do with it."

The mailman looked at the writing and scratched his chin for a moment before shaking his head.

"Not ours. No postmark. Doesn't look like UPS or FedEx, either. No marks at all."

"Well, could you take it with you? Maybe drop it off at the post office?"

"Nope. Sorry, Ma'am. If it's not ours, I can't do anything with it. Maybe you could run over to the address and leave it there. Be quite a drive, though." He shrugged his apology, already turning to walk away.

"Yeah. Well thanks anyway." Emily tucked the package under her arm and grabbed her coffee, heading back into the house where she dropped the box on her kitchen table. Refilling her mug, she perched on the edge of a chair and stared at the box for a long time, wondering just what she should do.

I'm sure as hell not driving all the way into the city for this shit. I have work to do, she thought. Then she smiled as an idea occurred to her.

Emily wandered down the hall to the spare room she'd converted into an office several years ago upon moving in. She sipped her coffee as her computer booted, then typed the name and address into a search engine. There were hundreds of hits, but she found a link halfway down the first page that looked promising. Crossing her fingers, she clicked it and watched as a website opened. It looked like some sort of voodoo or witchcraft store called Dominik's Dark Arts, and the address matched. There was a phone number listed just below the hours of operation.

She jotted the number down on a post-it note and carried it back to the dining room, retrieving her cell phone from the counter.

The phone rang four times before a machine answered, playing a pleasant male voice with soft wind chimes in the background.

"You have reached Dominik's Dark Arts. I'm sorry, but I will be out of town for the weekend. Normal store hours will resume on Monday. Have a Dark Day."

Emily waited for the beep before leaving her message.

"Hi Dominik, this is Emily Haven. There seems to have been a mix up and a package meant for you was left on my doorstep. I will keep hold of it for the weekend so nothing happens to it. Please call me at your earliest convenience and we will figure out how to rectify the situation." She left her cell number, said goodbye to the machine, and hung up.

At least that was over. It was Friday, so she would have the whole weekend to work on her projects before possibly having to make the long trek into the city. Heading back to the office, she thought about the name Dominik Bettancourt, wondering where she had heard it before. Shrugging it off, Emily started her work for the day.

She soon forgot all about the box on her table.

***

Emily Haven was the founder and executive editor of Night Haven Books, a small publishing house she had built from the ground up, spending the majority of her thirties making it a success. Now in its tenth year of publishing, the company had earned a respected recognition in the field and won some awards for superior achievement by a small publishing house. Employing thirty part-time editors from all over the country, she used email and the internet to put together books and a print-on-demand press to put those books into online bookstores. Two of her contracted authors had recently made the bestseller list and business couldn't be better. Her list of projects was long and always kept her awake late into the night.

Shortly after midnight, Emily sat at her desk, putting the finishing touches on an anthology she was formatting. The duplex was silent, the family next door asleep. Though it was a nice neighborhood and an expensive house, she could still hear the goings on next door when the kids were particularly rambunctious or their television was turned up too loud. She had even been embarrassed to hear them fight on a couple of occasions.

The sound of telephone startled her. Emily looked at her cell phone even though it was a regular ring she heard, not the jazzy ringer her cell was set to. She hadn't owned a landline in years.

It's too loud to be coming from next door, she thought.

Emily stood up and walked down the hall, the ringing growing louder as she went. Turning on the dining room light, she looked at the battered box on her table. The ringing seemed to be coming from within. Loathe to open someone else's mail, but also afraid the noise might wake the children next door, Emily was unsure of how to proceed.

There must be a cell phone in there. Maybe I could just slit the tape and shut the thing off. Then tape it back up again with no one the wiser.

Grabbing a steak knife out of the block on the counter, she sat down at the table and stared at the box for a moment, willing it to be silent. It continued to ring, the shrill noise loud in the calm night. She was going to have to open it. Emily sighed and went to work, using the tip of the blade to carefully puncture the tape and slice it away. Just as she opened the flaps, the box gave a final ring and fell silent. She considered just closing it back up.

What if it starts ringing again? Well, it's already open.

Emily reached gingerly into the box, encountering not a cell phone as she had expected, but something much larger. She grabbed it and pulled it out carefully, setting it on the counter. She was half right, it was indeed a phone, but one like she had never seen before. Roughly the size of an old rotary phone, the squat base appeared to be fashioned from a human skull, two milky grey stones glued into the eye sockets, and a realistic set of teeth grinned at her.

Resting on two brackets which were screwed into the top of the skull was the handset, half of a thigh bone with two disks affixed to the ends as a mouth and earpiece. The handset was attached to the body by what looked like a heavy braid of dark hair. She lifted it up and traced her fingers across the smooth surfaces. Obviously it couldn't be real bone, that wouldn't be legal, but the artist had done a great job of making the resin look authentic, down to the pale yellow hue and small pits across the surface. There were a couple of teeth missing, the eye sockets deep and dark behind the semi-transparent stones.

There was no way the thing could've really worked, with no jack to plug a phone line into, and no numbers or dial on the face, but it would certainly be a cool conversation piece for whoever owned it.

Emily wished for a second that it was hers; it would make a fine addition to her collection of strange artifacts in her office. It would look right at home with the hideous dolls, monster busts, and replicas of wooden stakes and silver bullets. She lifted the phone to put it back in the box, then nearly dropped it as it let out a shrill ring.

"What the fuck?" Setting the phone gently on the counter, Emily stared in disbelief as the gray stones in the eye sockets glowed an eerie red, fading and sparking in time with the shrill sound of the ringing phone.

No way. She thought, wondering for a moment if she had

fallen asleep while editing and was still slumped over her keyboard, having a strange dream. *It's not even plugged in.*

Emily cautiously picked up the handset, holding it up to her ear in a way that it didn't actually touch her face.

"Hello?"

There was a heavy hiss of static on the line before a gravelly male voice responded.

"Emily? Is that you, baby?"

A sob lodged in her throat. It was impossible.

"Daddy?"

"Oh baby! I miss you. It's been so long and I'm so lonely."

Hot tears gathered in her eyes, her knuckles white where she gripped the handset. She knew without a doubt it was her father's voice. It had been a quick and terrible death eight years ago when they found the lung cancer. Four months from diagnosis to burial, and she missed and grieved for him every day since.

"Oh Daddy. I miss you, too. I think about you every day. I wonder if you can see me, if you're proud of me. I love you so much."

"Proud of you? Are you kidding, girl? How could I possibly be proud of you?" His voice changed, darker, harsher.

Emily froze, her mouth moving but no sounds emerging as she struggled to make sense of the heartless words coming from her kind and loving and *dead* father.

"Just what the hell have you done to be proud of, you worthless bitch? Look at you. No man, no family. What good is a woman with no babies? Does your success keep you warm at night? Did you want to grow up to be a lonely old woman with no one to fuck? You sit alone all night, typing away at your damned computer, your cold, hateful womb empty and worthless. I bet your fucking ovaries are shriveled black grapes."

"Daddy?"

"Don't worry, Emily. There's a place in hell for you. For all you worthless, career-minded bitches who think you're too good for a man. To goddamned high-class to squeeze a baby out of your

rotten crotches. You'll love it here. You're gonna learn what a woman is really good for. They're gonna fuck you in ways you never knew they could. Maybe I'll take my turn and give those dried up ovaries a stir!"

The skull phone made a loud crash as it hit the wall, knocking a decent hole in the plaster, but Emily no longer cared if she woke the neighbors.

***

"Calm down, Em. There's got to be some logical explanation. Someone's just fucking with you is all."

"I don't know how." Emily drew a steadying breath, trying hard not to cry anymore. She had done plenty of that already as she relayed the horrifying details of the night before to Layla, her only sister. Her cell phone felt hot against her face.

"I know you said you looked, but it was late. There had to be some hidden battery compartment or something. Some remote microphone in the thing."

"So how did they know what Dad's voice sounded like, Layla?"

"Maybe they didn't. Maybe you were just thinking about Dad. We all miss him, honey. Maybe you were just missing him extra bad and your mind made you hear what you wanted to hear."

"Well I sure as shit didn't want to hear *that.*" Emily snapped.

"I know. That's not what I'm saying. It's a sick prank. You must've pissed someone off. Where's the phone now? Maybe you should take it to the police." Layla was always a calming influence, had a way of making those around her feel at ease regardless of the situation.

"I threw it in the box and drove into the city. Took me two hours to find the place in the middle of the night, but I did. Left it right on the sidewalk in front of the guy's store. I don't care if it gets stolen. Whoever takes it will probably bring it back, anyway. I should've never called that guy and left the message. Now he's gonna get pissed at me for not keeping it. Fucking store looked creepy too, all kinds of voodoo and witchcraft shit in the windows."

"Hey now. You're into that shit." Layla laughed and soon Emily found herself chuckling as well.

"I don't *believe* in it. I just like scary movies and horror novels. It's not the same as living it."

"Well, Big Sis, maybe you need a vacation. Robby and the kids and I would love to have you."

With the subject changed, they talked for a few minutes about how long it had been since they'd seen one another and the cost of plane tickets from New York City to L.A. Layla refused to let Emily go until she had extracted a tentative promise that when things slowed down, Emily would visit them in California. Though she tried to remain upbeat after the conversation, Emily couldn't help but feel awful for the rest of the day. The echo of her father's words seemed louder when she compared her sister's family to her own solitary life. It certainly wasn't the first time she had questioned the decisions she'd made, but this time they seemed to have more of a dire relevance.

***

Emily woke from a nightmare she couldn't hold onto. Something about hell and babies screaming. Children who ran from her when she tried to save them from the flames. She lay in her bed, disoriented in the darkness for a moment before the sound that woke her came again.

Ringing.

From the kitchen.

"No way. No fucking way," she croaked as she slid out of bed and crept down the hall. Emily knew what she would find when she turned on the light, but was powerless to contain a shriek when she saw the phone sitting on the counter, its eyes glowing red with every ring.

Backing away, she kept her eyes on it, not looking away as her back encountered the heavy front door. She felt if the locks were still engaged. They were, and the chain was still in place.

None of this is happening. I'm dreaming this time. There's no way it's back.

Eyes burning with a demonic light, it continued to trill, as if mocking her. Emily remembered Layla's assurance that this was a cruel prank, and her fear turned to anger at whoever could be vile enough to do this to her. Before she lost her nerve, she marched over to the counter and grabbed the handset, yelling into the mouth piece.

"You're not my fucking father!"

There was a hiss of static once again, the voice on the other side sounding amused when it replied.

"Of course I'm not your father, babe. It's Ricky."

Emily froze, her blood cold in her veins. It sounded like Ricky. It really did. But like her father, Ricky was dead.

"Prove it."

"Oh baby. I know things about you that no one else does. Your first time was with me in my parents' bed when they left town for the weekend. You made me wait a year and a half before you gave in. You cried when I was done."

It was Ricky.

Ricky had been Emily's boyfriend from Sophomore year of high school until her Freshman year of college. He was a grade behind her, and she had thought they could bear to be parted for one year until he graduated and joined her at the state university. It all came to an end when he plowed his sports car into the back of a semi-truck at sixty miles per hour, taking his head off and severely injuring her sister Layla, who had leaned over at just the right moment to retrieve a can of pop that had spilled on the floor.

Emily had wondered for a long time if something might have been going on between Layla and Ricky, but her sister swore that he was just giving her a ride home from cheerleading practice. In the end, Emily chose to believe her sister, though in weak moments she still wondered.

"What do you want?"

"Wow, babe. You sure don't seem too happy to hear from me. Of course, you always were a frigid cunt."

"I'm not listening to this. Do you hear me? I'm hanging up, you sick bastard. I *will not listen to this!*" Emily yelled into the phone, rage and fear making her shake.

"Oh yes you will! You will because you want to know. You NEED to know what happened. You will listen until I'm done

talking, bitch. You think we would've gotten married, don't you? You think we were some perfect fucking couple. Well, we weren't, Em. We never were. I was putting the stones to baby sis for a year before you even let me get a finger in you. You were a cold bitch, but Layla was hot for it. That little slut couldn't wait to betray you. You think you're so close? Little sister was slobbering all over my cock every fucking time you turned your back. And you know what? She was good at it, too. Better than you'll ever be."

Emily surprised herself by gently replacing the receiver in the cradle. She looked around the room with a calmness she didn't feel. After rummaging in some drawers, she finally found something she could use. Just like the night before, she packed up the phone and put the box in the trunk of her car, though this time she headed away from the city. After some time, she pulled over alongside a vacant field, leaving her hazard lights flashing.

It was easier to destroy than she imagined. The hammer blows broke the bone (she no longer entertained thoughts it was anything other than real bone), shattering it into large pieces she then smashed again. She didn't stop until the sun peeked over the horizon and nothing but white dust and two gray stones remained of the phone. Grabbing her smokes off the dash, she lit one, then held her lighter to the cord of braided hair that had connected the handset to the body. When nothing was left to break or burn, Emily drove back home and fell into bed, spending the rest of the morning in a dreamless slumber.

***

Emily felt miserable. Sitting on her couch in front of the television, she stared at the screen, not watching it. Layla was on a plane, heading to New York to assist her with the hell she found herself plunged into, but it didn't make her feel any better. Rather than being encouraged by her sister's act of loyalty and her insistence that this was not something she could handle alone, Emily felt disturbed.

Why was Layla's reaction stronger to a phone call from Ricky? What was with the heavy silence after I told her what Ricky said about her? Emily's thoughts chased themselves around her head, long buried doubts resurfacing to nag at her mind. *Was it true?*

The microwave beeped, informing Emily that her coffee from last night was reheated. She shuffled into the kitchen, and catching sight of her reflection in the black glass of the appliance, she let out a harsh laugh.

"You look like shit, old girl." Grabbing the mug, she poured some expensive vanilla creamer in and returned to the couch.

It was all ridiculous, really. This business of a bone phone just *showing up* to bring her calls from the dead. But ridiculous or not, it still happened. Emily wondered why she wasn't spending more time contemplating the impossibility of her situation, rather than chewing over recurring doubts about the one man she had ever truly loved and her only sibling whom she thought shared all of her secrets with her.

These things shouldn't matter anymore. I'm tired, she thought. *Getting calls in the middle of the night from dead loved ones will do that to you.*

Layla was due to land in two hours, and Emily had just enough time to shower before she drove to the airport. Heaving a sigh, she got up from the couch and went into the bathroom to start the water. Undressed, she stood before the mirror, her gaze drawn to every imperfection in the glass.

When did I get this extra fat around my middle? And where did these sagging breasts come from? Or all this gray hair? She couldn't remember the last time she had gone for a run, something she had done regularly in college but seemed to always be too busy for now. Her youth was passing. Maybe her dad was right. *No! That wasn't my dad. He would never say such hateful things.*

The hot water restored her mood somewhat. As she toweled dry, Emily looked in the mirror once again, forcing herself to find things that still looked good. She wasn't gorgeous but she still looked okay, and was smart and funny. She still had plenty to offer someone, should that someone ever arrive.

Dressed for the day, with her hair wound up in a towel, she

padded into the kitchen for a fresh cup of coffee. She yelped and braced a hand on the doorframe, afraid for a moment she might faint.

"Goddamn you!" Emily stood in the doorway, her heart hammering. The phone sat quietly on the counter, no sign of the damage she'd inflicted on it the night before.

The eyes glowed hellishly red just seconds before it started to ring. Emily dreaded the call, but was powerless to keep herself from answering it.

"Hello?"

"Hey sis." Layla's voice came through clearly.

"Nice try. You can't be my sister. She's still *alive."*

"Correction Em, I was alive. But as usual, you fucked everything up and now I'm dead. Turn on the news if you don't believe me."

"Alright." Emily changed the channel on the television, turning up the volume just in time to catch the breaking news that a plane had crashed on the runway at JFK. There were no known survivors. She didn't need to look up her sister's flight number to know she'd been on it. "Oh, Jesus."

"Jesus has nothing to do with this, Em. I would still be alive if you hadn't fucked with the wrong person, just like Ricky would probably still be alive if we hadn't been forced to hide everything. You selfish twat. You fuck up everything. Thinking you're so smart and better than everyone else."

"Stop. You aren't Layla. My sister loved me." Emily felt the tears come. Not her sister. Not her baby sister.

"Oh please. You know it's me. And you know I was fucking Ricky. Everyone knew it, but you were just too damned stubborn to see it. If you would've just let him go we could've been fucking in a bed, not racing down the highway at sixty-five with his cock in my mouth. That's why I survived. There wasn't any spilled pop can that distracted us. I was sucking him off. And you know what? The last thing he did was cum in my mouth. His eyes were closed because he was cumming in my mouth! That's why he hit the truck. You worthless bitch. I hated you for that. Sitting beside my

hospital bed, trying to hide your grief over Ricky because you were worried about me. I hated how weak you were. You still are."

"Shut up. Just shut the fuck up! You aren't Layyyyla!" Emily dropped the phone, but she could still hear Layla's voice.

"See ya tonight sissy. I'll tell you about all the things that Ricky liked to do to me. The things you wouldn't let him do. We'll talk about all the good old times. It'll be a blast!"

***

Emily sat in a hotel room, a half empty bottle of vodka beside her. She'd stopped by the liquor store on her way to the hotel. Being sober wasn't an option. Too much grief and fear for that.

A phone rang. Emily started, her eyes darting around the room in search of the demonic skull. Realizing it was her cell phone, she let out a nervous chuckle. Checking the number to make sure it wasn't her Mom again, she saw a number she didn't recognize.

"Hello?"

"Hello." A man's deep voice spoke. It sounded cultured, containing a light undertone of some unidentifiable accent. "Is this Emily?"

"Speaking. Who is this?"

"This is Dominik Bettancourt. You left me a message saying you had something that you believed belonged to me. I'm sorry; I just got back to town a few hours ago."

Emily felt her pulse quicken, bolting upright on her chair and gripping the phone until her knuckles cracked.

"Oh, thank God! Mr. Bettancourt. I need your help."

"Yes, I'm certain you do. Do you still have the phone?" His voice was soothing.

"No. I left it at home. There's something wrong with that thing. Something evil. You wouldn't believe what's happened to me in the last couple days."

"You might be surprised, Emily, at what I would believe. You said the phone was at home. I take it you are not?"

"No. I drove into town and got a room at the Marriot. Please, could you meet me here? We could go together and get your phone."

"That won't be necessary, Ms. Haven. The phone will show up on its own. And it's not mine. It's *yours.*" His tone grew cool.

"Please, Mr. Bettancourt! You have to help me, I'm begging you."

"Begging me? Isn't that rich. How many have begged *you*, Emily? I wonder how many dreams you have crushed of those who have sent you their work, only to be given a *form letter rejection*. Why would I help *you*? I'm the one who sent the phone." He laughed then, deep and throaty.

"You sent the phone? Why? What did I ever do to you? I don't even know you." Emily felt deep dread sink into her chest.

"It'll come to you, Ms. Haven. Enjoy your hell. I'm sure there's something special waiting for you."

***

The phone call came around one in the morning. Drunk and unable to hold it any longer, Emily staggered into the bathroom to pee, returning to find the phone sitting on the desk. She answered on the first ring, resigned from the stress and intoxication to see this through to the end, but still dreading the voice on the other line.

Will it be my mom? How many will die before this is over? I've killed Layla; please don't let it be Mom, too.

"Who is it?"

"It's me, Emily. Who else would it be?"

Emily thought she was immune to the shock, no longer really believed that the phone calls could surprise her. How many times had she heard this voice on answering machine recordings and video tapes, at once recognizing who it was and at the same time refusing to believe the voice that sounded so different when she spoke was hers?

"It's me. It's you. And it's just about over, girl."

"But I'm not dead." Emily whispered, her head swimming with vodka and shock.

"Yes you are. You just don't know it yet."

"Please." She sobbed, her voice coming out in a whine. "No more. What could I have done to deserve this?"

"Oh, you deserve it all right. Think back. You knew his name from somewhere. Dominik Bettancourt. He was a writer. Years ago when you first started publishing. He sent a story for one of your contests. It wasn't very good, but it was the best he could do. You rejected it. Sent a form letter. Do you remember?"

"I do now. I rejected his story. But it wasn't good. Not everyone can be good." Despite the surreal experience of speaking to herself on the phone, Emily did remember him now. And his story. Some wretched tale of voodoo with little plot and poor grammar. She *had* to reject it.

"But you didn't just reject it, did you? Oh no. You had to use him as an example of what not to do. You read his story to your friends so you could all laugh at his attempts. You put excerpts on your blog, cleverly disguised, but you let everyone mock him. It was humiliating for him. He gave up on writing. Gave up on the dreams he'd had since he was a child. You and your friends destroyed something inside of him and what grew in its place was hate."

"I did. I did all of it. I'm sorry. I'm so fucking sorry. I was young and didn't know much about professionalism. I would never do that to him now. Please. One more chance. I'll make it up to him. I promise." Emily sobbed, her shame and fear overwhelming.

She had done all those things, using this man as an anecdote at countless cocktail parties. Long after she'd forgotten his name, she would still mention his awful story, using it to make others laugh. It was a horrible thing to do to someone, but she would've never dreamed in a million years the man would find out. That he would have otherworldly ways of finding out.

"You are already making it up to him with your suffering. Your pain is his comfort when he sleeps at night. Enough talk. It's time. They are all waiting for you down here. Oh the things they have to show you. Come home, Emily. Come home."

There was a click on the line, then nothing. Not even a dial tone or open air. Emily sat with the bone to her ear, now nothing more than a prop. A novelty for the desk she would never see again. Setting the handset back in its cradle, she picked the whole thing up in one hand and carried it to the balcony. The night air felt chilly when she opened the doors, a brisk reminder that fall was coming, with winter close behind. Looking over the railing, she could see traffic racing by below despite the late hour.

Ten stories up, she wondered if she'd hear it hit the sidewalk. She doubted it. Emily tossed the phone over the edge without another thought, realizing at the last second that she might hit a pedestrian, but no longer really caring. She probably wouldn't survive the night, had no doubt a legion of demons would soon be beating down the door to carry her off to hell, and killing a stranger wouldn't matter much. She listened for the sound of the crash, or horns honking and people yelling, but heard nothing.

Emily frowned and looked over the railing. Nothing had changed below. Had it even hit the ground? Did it disappear on the way down, only to materialize behind her on the desk? Glancing over her shoulder, she could see nothing in her suite, so she stepped onto the bottom rail and leaned over, craning her neck to see if the phone lay smashed on the sidewalk. The rail gave way without a sound, no screeching protest of metal, no squealing of iron bars. It simply let loose, pitching her into the cold air.

Time seemed to expand and contract at the same time as her body hurtled toward the earth, her screams trailing into the night and rousing hotel guests from their slumber and onto balconies in their pajamas. The fall was endless, but over in just seconds as the asphalt rushed towards her face, people on the street stopping to watch, crying out as her body fell headfirst to the ground.

Emily saw none of this, neither people nor the concrete waiting to embrace her and crush her body to fragments and jelly. As she fell, the fires of hell opened up beneath her, a blast of heat drying her tears as she plummeted towards her father, Ricky, and Layla, their arms opened to receive her. Witnesses would report that just before the woman hit the ground, her body splattering a ten-foot radius, she appeared to be smiling with opened arms, as if in an embrace.

***

Stew Swenson couldn't sleep. He'd lain in bed tossing and turning all night, troubled by the news he'd received the day before. Though they were in many ways competitors, both of them running small horror publishing houses, Stew had met Emily years ago at a convention and they'd become fast friends. The news of her death, still being investigated as a suicide, had hit him pretty hard. He gave up on sleep and slipped into his pants, putting on a pair of slippers to head outside.

The Florida surf was indescribably beautiful at sunrise and he hoped it would help quell the grief in his heart. Pouring a cup of coffee, he opened the screen door and stepped outside, tripping over something on the way out. A beat up box lay next to his door, covered in massive loops of packing tape.

"What the hell?" He picked it up, reading the jagged writing on the top. No return address, just a name and a New York City address. *How the hell did you get here?* It was much too early for mail delivery and there were no postal markings on the box, anyhow. Someone must've hand delivered the box. Stew set it on the table and sat down on his porch swing, his brow furrowed in concentration. "Dominik Bettancourt. Now where do I know that name?"

SISTER ALICE'S SUITOR

PLOP!

Alice leaned forward on the toilet. A wriggle of white had caught her attention and she looked down at the crotch of her panties pushed to her knees. A plump white worm stuck to the cotton, its eyeless front searching the air for food.

Oh God! Oh my God! It's a maggot!

Alice dropped to her knees and turned to face the toilet, bile burning her throat as she leaned into the bowl to retch. She sat back and tried to hold it in at the last moment, but vomit splattered over her gown and onto the pristine bathroom floor. Clamping a hand across her mouth, she choked back a sob and fought a fresh wave of nausea, her eyes bulging out of her pale face. Cold sweat ran between her shoulder blades and she began to shake.

I'm dying and I can't tell anyone!

She closed her eyes and prayed it would all go away. She opened them again, peered into the bowl, and shrank back at the sight. Dozens of maggots floated amongst her partially digested lunch, but they hadn't come out of her mouth.

A band of pain tightened around her midsection, and she let out an involuntary *Oooh!* The labor was starting.

Alice crawled haltingly across the tile into her bedroom and pressed her face against the plush carpet as another ferocious contraction hit. She kicked off her nasty panties without a second thought. As the pain eased, she felt a half-hearted kick, causing her inexplicable panic.

She hadn't wanted this pregnancy, had been so horrified by the circumstances behind the conception that she told no one these last nine months, secretly hoping she would miscarry. She had even tried to abort it herself with herbs and drugs, but to no avail. As the pregnancy progressed, as she grew larger and felt the infant stirring in her womb, Alice felt an attachment forming. She felt a mother's love stir within her, causing her to abandon her quest to terminate the pregnancy. She feared for the baby now. What if the baby didn't make it? What if she had damaged it? She knew this child wasn't natural, but it didn't matter. She loved it. No matter what it turned out to be, she would care for it and love it as a mother should. No one would take it from her. No one. She would kill for her child, with her bare hands if necessary.

Her baby would survive.

Alice clawed her way up the comforter and onto the bed where she laid back on the pillows and clutched at her swollen abdomen. The pains came quick and hard, and she tried to breathe shallowly through them like she read in the childbirth books, but it was difficult not to pant.

She clumsily peeled off her gown and spread her hands across her distended belly. Mottled, dark patches that had appeared months ago had now spread into a horribly bruised mass of purple and black flesh, tight, shiny, and somehow putrid looking, like the lividity of a week old corpse.

Her contractions became relentless.

Alice's water broke with an alarming pop and foul smelling amniotic fluid gushed from between her thighs; her white sheets were now the dirty grey of used mop water. In the late afternoon sunlight, she could see the gleam of dark clots of blood and slimy, green mucus pooling on the sheets. She screamed as another cramp struck, leaning her head back and squeezing her eyes shut.

With her eyes closed in the half-trance of childbirth, Alice remembered back to a night nine months ago. As sick as it was, whenever she was overwhelmed she sought comfort in that night.

***

Alice earned the nickname "Sister Alice" decades before in college, being the last virgin in her dorm. Coeds had wagered on when she might give it up, most of them placing their money on never—a bet they would've won.

At forty-five, she was the stereotypical, dowdy librarian. Despite her mousy features, she perfected a stern countenance which silenced the rowdiest group of teens with merely a glance. Her work was her life. She returned home every night to a spinster's cottage located on the edge of town. Small and tidy, she decorated it with doilies on nearly every surface and kept company with six cats. She had no other friends and nothing in the way of a social life. Her only living family was Sheila, a younger sister, happily married with three children and living across the country in New Hampshire.

On the verge of menopause, Alice had long ago given up on having a family of her own, something she had always desperately wanted. She was now content with her solitude and with her simple life. It didn't even bother her that her romantic life was non-existent. She hadn't had a real date since college, and even then, the captain of the chess club had quickly broken up with her, accusing her of being frigid and dull. Her lack of prospects was a subject that Sheila never failed to harp about in their bi-monthly phone conversations.

The phone calls were always the same. In the first half hour, Sheila would dominate with tales of her children and their various activities. Alice would struggle to sound interested and amused as Sheila recounted how well the oldest had done at her dance recital and how Junior had once again shoved peas up his nose. Then for about ten minutes Sheila would gush about her husband Frank and whatever wonderful thing he'd done for her lately, while Alice silently endured with gritted teeth. The conversation would then turn to Alice's activities and Sheila questioning whether or not she had met any interesting men. This always led to at least fifteen minutes of Alice defending herself against her sister's well-meant prying. Finally, it would end in an uncomfortable silence with terse goodbyes.

It had been a particularly hard day and Alice had so far consumed a half a bottle of red wine after coming home—something she rarely did—when the scheduled phone call came. She continued to drink while Sheila chatted on, and she was quite drunk when the conversation took the inevitable turn towards her own sorry, single existence.

"I just don't know why you don't do anything social, Alice. You certainly aren't going to find Mr. Right sitting behind a desk all day, cataloguing dusty, old books."

"Maybe there is no Mr. Right for me. Have you ever thought about that?" Alice felt proud that her voice carried only a hint of a slur. "Besides, I'm very busy at the library right now. I wouldn't even have time to date if I wanted to."

"But don't you want to? I mean, I hate the idea of you festering away in that house all by yourself with nothing but those mangy cats for company! You need interaction, human interaction!"

"My cats are not mangy!" Alice snapped. "And has it ever occurred to you that maybe I don't want a husband and kids? Maybe I don't like goddamned children?!"

Sheila was silent for a while, and Alice felt instantly sorry as she searched for the right words to apologize when Sheila spoke again in a softer tone.

"I will pray for you, Alice. It's all I can do. Maybe God can heal your bitter heart by bringing a wonderful man into your life."

This was the final straw. Having also been deeply religious her entire life, but now drunk and furious at Sheila's presumptions and meddling, Alice gripped the phone and spoke through tightly clenched teeth, words flowing out of her mouth before she could even consider the lack of wisdom behind them.

"You just go ahead and pray to God. Because I'm not going to.

He hasn't done a damn thing for me in that area. I think I will pray to the devil tonight; maybe he will send me a man."

Alice hung up the phone without another word, hot tears of shame and regret stinging the backs of her eyes, and finished her bottle of wine in one long pull before stumbling off to bed. As her eyelids closed, the sound of her sister's voice echoed in her mind. She flinched at the recollection of her own hostile words and pressed her eyelids tightly together to block them out. Soon enough, her persistence and the bottle of wine she'd had helped her off to the Land of Nod where a dream awaited her. A vivid dream. A sexual dream.

***

Alice was in the garden, the warm August mist thick around her body, obscuring her from passersby on the street. She had no memory of getting out of bed to come here, or of removing her gown and sensible panties. But here she stood. Bare to the world.

She ran her hands over her breasts, delighting in the moist feel of condensation on her flesh. Suddenly, she was aroused by the act of being so brazen, so nude in a place where she could be easily discovered. Her palm slid down her slightly doughy belly to tease between her thighs.

The mist parted and a young man stood before her in the haze, his pale, naked body glistening in the glimmer of the moonlight. No more than twenty, he was beautiful.

Alice's eyes followed the muscled indentation of his hip as it curved deliciously toward his cock, which stood in impressive arousal. Her eyes widened. Despite his fierce erection, his skin lacked the flush of sex. Instead, his flesh was an unhealthy shade of grey, his eyes milky and unblinking marbles, and his throat opened from ear to ear in a grisly and gashed grin. She could see knobby cartilage in the mostly bloodless wound on his neck as her eyes took him in from head to toe.

For all his youthful sexuality, the man before her was obviously dead.

The sight of him should have sent Alice screaming into the

night. But she did not fear him. She felt unable to resist placing her palm upon the cold, hard muscles that formed the ridge of his abdomen. It surprised her when he unexpectedly fell over, landing on his back with a meaty thud, his glazed eyes moving slowly up to her.

Stunned by this turn of events, Alice knelt by his side, the warm night air caressing her body as her eyes moved from his, and rested on his erection. A jolt of sexual awareness sizzled between her thighs. She knew she should be horrified by the feeling, disgusted by the corpse that lay before her, but she couldn't quell her arousal. Years of burying her sexuality beneath the mundane details of life, came crashing down on her, causing a hunger that needed fulfillment, despite the morbid circumstances.

Up this close, she could smell him, a rotten, yet slightly sweet aroma. She still felt an overwhelming need to feel that rigid, young flesh inside her. She had no idea how his penis could be erect with no blood flow, but didn't care. Instead she marveled at the thick, sturdy veins that ran darkly beneath the bluish skin.

He was dead, but he was here, and he was hers! Leave it to the devil to deliver a dead man to her door. Even in her dream she had vague recollections of issuing that challenge, and she would take what she could get. Finally she could know the carnal bliss of coupling with a man. She could experience all the pleasure that the girls in the dorm had moaned about, taunting her mercilessly.

Alice moved to straddle the boy, her hand caressing the silky, hard skin of his cock. It was cold as she guided it slowly into her own hot flesh; the delicious feeling of stretching to accommodate him caused her to groan aloud with pleasure.

He didn't move, but remained erect, allowing her to slide and grind against him, building her own pace, her hands clawing at chilly, hard pectoral muscles. She wished he would touch her breasts, but his arms remained stiff at his sides, so she grabbed them herself, fondling and pinching her own nipples with abandon as she felt her orgasm approaching. Alice continued to ride him, rocking hard as her climax crashed over her in exquisite waves that seemed endless. He made an odd garbled sound, like a choked moan, and then his cock moved, spasming inside her as it gushed forth, flooding her insides with cold semen.

***

Alice slept in the morning after the dream until well after ten, the mid-morning light streaming through the blinds, assaulting her eyes. She hadn't slept this late in years, but it was Sunday, her day off, so it didn't matter.

Her head hurt from all the wine, but she felt a pleasant throbbing in her groin, and debated on whether to get up at all. Her thighs felt sticky, and she vaguely remembered her erotic dream.

Must've been a real doozy.

Throwing back the covers, she felt stunned to realize she was naked, having shed her sleeping garments in the night. Her hand flew up to her mouth and she uttered a horrified shriek when her gaze fell to her thighs. Opaque in places, a thick, black slime coated her skin from crotch to knee.

It smelled like dead fish rotting in the sun.

Alice jumped from her bed and ran to the adjacent bathroom, turning the water as hot as she could handle before scrubbing her body. She continued to wash long after the filth was gone, grunting out harsh sobs and shaking with disgust. Her mind refused to accept that the episode had been anything more than a perverse dream, despite the evidence that swirled down the drain. She got out and threw the soiled washcloths (it had taken three to remove all traces of the foul slime on her thighs) into the trash.

Wearing an old t-shirt and jeans, she had just begun stripping the linen from her bed when there was a knock at her door. She froze, suddenly nervous. No one ever came to her house. She debated ignoring it, her hair was still wet and she hadn't bothered to put on a bra, so intent was she on cleaning up the bed. The knock came again, more insistent this time, and she went to answer.

A young man in a suit stood on her porch, his badge gleaming in the afternoon sunlight when he held it out for her inspection. He smiled at her, but it didn't touch his eyes. Alice stared, wondering why a police officer was at her door.

Must be official business.

He cleared his throat and spoke. "I'm sorry to bother you. Miss . . . "

"Collins. Alice Collins."

"Ms. Collins. I am Detective Dunlavy and I'm here in response to a call from a pedestrian that saw something in your garden this morning when he was walking his dog."

The detective had a pleasant manner, but his eyes were sharp, scrutinizing her reaction. She hoped she didn't appear nervous, and really had no reason to be since she didn't know what he was talking about. Bits and pieces of her dream started creeping into her head and she felt a little ill.

"So what was in my garden, officer?" She tried to gain confidence by using her no-nonsense librarian voice, but inside trembled with fear. Alice felt detached from the situation, complex emotions warring within her, but surprisingly calm on the outside.

"Not was, Ms. Collins. There is a body in your garden."

"What? You can't be serious! How would a body wind up in my garden?" Alice felt as though she might faint.

The dream! Oh the damn dream! What have I done?

She stumbled and the young detective caught her arm, then led her into the living room and sat her on the couch as he disappeared into the kitchen for a glass of water. When he returned, his accusatory look was gone.

He must now believe that I had nothing to do with this. Alice knew she wasn't out of the woods yet, because there would be an investigation, and she'd naturally be a suspect. The officer stood a few feet away, watching her sip her water.

"I'm sorry to have to tell you this news, ma'am."

"Was the person murdered?" Alice asked, her eyes wide with wonder, certain that she had somehow wound up on the other side of the looking glass.

"Well that's the weird thing," the young officer shifted his feet, obviously uncomfortable. "He was murdered. But we already know who did it. This boy was murdered two days ago by his roommate in a dorm at the college."

"My Lord!" Alice exclaimed. "I know what you're talking about! That poor boy whose roommate slit his throat while he was sleeping. I heard about that! Dreadful business. I work at the college in the library; and, well, you know how young people gossip. So how did he end up in my garden?"

"That's what we're trying to figure out, Ms. Collins. His body was reported missing from the morgue last night. There were some legal issues with the family and we were holding him for an autopsy, but they didn't want one performed. Then last night, he just disappears and shows up in your garden this morning."

"Why my yard?" Alice was genuinely perplexed, though she had a terrible suspicion the cop was way off with his theory. She was starting to believe that something much more sinister had brought the corpse to her property.

"I don't know for sure. Have you had any problems with a particular student?"

"None that stand out in my mind."

"How about last night. Did you hear anything unusual?"

"No, I'm sorry. I was asleep." Her eyes darted to the empty wine bottle and the cop looked as well, a small smile curling his mouth in understanding.

Well, better for him to think I'm a drunk than a necrophiliac, Alice thought.

Detective Dunlavy didn't miss Alice's nervous behavior or the signs of alcohol consumption from the night before. There was no surveillance footage from the morgue, though the technicians had yet to find any evidence that the cameras had been tampered with. He had a suspicion that this was some sort of prank played out by college students on the quiet librarian, but he remained alert as he questioned her, looking for indications that she may have been involved somehow. He was certain that the murder was solved, the roommate had confessed to the crime and the evidence didn't point to any alternative, but he still had to investigate this disturbing twist in the case.

The detective stayed a while longer, interviewing her as to her whereabouts both last evening and the night of the murder, before taking an official statement from Alice. The coroner's office took care of removing the body. She didn't go look at it, didn't want to see it and confirm her terrible suspicions. Detective Dunlavy left with an apology and a promise to be in touch soon. Alice watched him go, then locked the door behind him, her knees trembling so badly she collapsed right there in the foyer and wept.

Detective Dunlavy contacted Alice three more times over the next month, hoping she would remember some scrap of a detail that might help their investigation, but she could offer him nothing. The young man's family buried him, and life went on. With no plausible leads on the case, it was soon put aside and mostly forgotten. The young man who killed the student had been diagnosed with schizophrenia and institutionalized. Alice didn't care at all about the case or how the body had come to be in her yard. She knew the terrible truth. She had more important things to worry about.

That month she missed her period.

***

Alice ignored it at first, figured that maybe she was beginning menopause, though she'd been showing none of the usual signs that her menstrual cycle was winding down. This had to be some horrible dream.

Corpses do not walk into your garden with the intent to copulate, and they certainly don't knock you up in the process!

She considered calling to make an appointment with her doctor the next day, but she didn't. She was afraid of what they might find, certain that within her remained evidence of her vile indiscretion and they would lock her away forever in some asylum. Once she was forced to divulge the horrendous details behind the conception, the obstetrician's next call would certainly be to a psychiatrist. She couldn't go to a doctor, or rather, she knew on some level that she *wouldn't* go to the doctor. She prayed the symptoms would go away.

During the earlier part of the pregnancy, Alice had spent a good deal of time researching abortion on the internet, ordering countless herbal medicines that promised to terminate the child "gently and naturally". None had worked.

Bouts of severe nausea and cramping left her weak for days, but the child still seemed to thrive. It was hopeless. She would have to see this to the end or die trying. Alice wondered what the cops would say if they found her body. Oh, the horror this would create within the community when they discovered whatever monster she gestated in her diseased womb.

***

She spent the next couple months trying to do her job, ignoring the morning sickness and fatigue, pretending she just had the flu. When her swelling abdomen became too much to cover with clothes, Alice took a hiatus from work, claiming mental exhaustion after the stress from the prank in her garden. After decades of working at the same college, she had reached tenure, and with no family and simple tastes, her savings were more than enough to support her. With no friends and her sister so far away, there were no visitors to check on her, which was just how she liked it.

Alone in her house, Alice could no longer pretend she wasn't pregnant. There had been no test to confirm it, but she had all the usual symptoms. She grew larger every day; and, at around six months along, the thing within her began to squirm, making her want to tear her belly open and rip it out.

There were other symptoms, as well. Patches of dark bruising appeared on her abdomen that spread fast, forming mottled patterns all over her torso, resembling some kind of fungus. Her teeth began rotting nearly overnight, turning dark and mossy before falling out of gums which bled almost daily.

And there was her appetite. Alice knew that expectant mothers often craved strange foods, sometimes even inedible things like soil or egg shells. She was still pretty sure her cravings were over the top. She became sick when eating fruits and vegetables, so she was stuck with dairy, meats, and breads. Then she could only drink milk that had long since curdled. She would wait for the mold to grow on her cheese and bread and relish in its musty green flavor as if it were the sweetest ambrosia.

The worst, though, was the meat. She often left raw steaks and hamburgers on the counter for days, gnawing on them once they changed from a ruby red to a greenish grey. These things should have poisoned her, should have at the very least made her quite ill, but they tasted better to her than a pint of rocky road ice cream.

As terrible as those things were, they were nothing compared to her odor. By the time she reached the seventh month, Alice could no longer go out in public at all. Her horrible pallor and nearly toothless mouth looked bad, but her stink was unbearable. She gave up on trying to find different soaps and deodorants to control it, and douching was useless. No matter what, she always smelled ripe and gamy, like a dead animal. She thought she might be dying. Alice ordered her necessities online, instructing the deliverymen to leave it all on the porch. She wondered if they could smell her through the door.

Perhaps driven away by the smell, even her cats wanted nothing to do with her, half of them having run off and never returned. The remaining three spent most of their time hiding from her, and only ventured out of their hidey-holes to eat. They'd abandon dinner completely and scamper away when she tried to touch them.

***

Alice broke down and made an appointment with an obstetrician. In the waiting room, the other women shied away from her, clearly trying to hide their disgust, but failing miserably. Even the receptionist turned her head away from Alice when they spoke, attempting to escape her pungent body odor.

The doctor flinched when he saw her, and Alice thought she heard him gag during the pelvic examination.

"Alice, at your age and given the lack of prenatal care, I would suggest an ultrasound and genetic testing." The doctor said.

"I will take the ultrasound for now, but I need to think about further testing."

Alice's palms were sweating and her mind raced, wondering what the testing would reveal. She lay back on the table and closed her eyes as the doctor spread a thick jelly on her stomach, pressing a round instrument against her and squinting at the image on the screen of the mobile ultrasound machine. He shook his head and grunted, going over the same spot multiple times. When he had wiped her belly and helped her back into a seated position, he looked at her sadly, obviously unhappy with the news he was about to give her.

"Is it alive?" she asked, her blunt and emotionless manner taking the doctor by surprise.

"There is a heartbeat, but it seems irregular. There were also, some . . . abnormalities . . . structural abnormalities that I'm concerned about. I feel that it would be in your best interest to proceed with genetic testing and amniocentesis at this point."

Alice was silent for a moment before nodding curtly. "I understand your concerns doctor. You have given me a lot to think about. I will need a day or two to decide what I want to do."

Leaving the doctor with a promise to call within the next day, Alice drove home and sat on her couch, a carton of spoiled milk on the table before her. She imagined herself undergoing the testing. The long needle puncturing her womb to draw forth a black, viscous fluid. As if it could read her mind, the baby kicked. She rubbed her belly, soothing it unconsciously. The baby responded to her gentle touch, ceasing its restless motion.

Alice felt a pang of unexpected affection for the creature. She didn't know what it would be, but despite its paternity, it was hers. She began to feel a begrudging respect for the little creature that refused to be destroyed. As her mind started to go, that respect turned into affection.

Fearful of what the tests might show, Alice called the doctor's office the next day and said she would be seeking treatment from a different obstetrician. It was a lie. She now knew that she would deal with whatever lay ahead, alone. Taken by surprise by the developing love she felt for the baby, she would let no one stop her from seeing this through to the end.

***

Alice threw herself back on the bed, cords of tendons sticking out on her neck while her clawing hands tangled in the bed sheets. Greasy sweat coated her body and bloody milk dribbled from her nipples as she choked back screams, terrified one of the neighbors would hear her and call the cops.

She dug her heals into the mattress. Her legs opened wide, pushing with all she was worth. She was going on pure instinct now, an animal reacting to the pain of birth. The agony was overwhelming and became her whole world as she struggled to expel the infant, fearing she would split right down the middle and bleed to death on her own bed. This excruciatingly long process sapped her strength.

Hearing her own flesh tear, Alice wailed, all thoughts of her neighbors calling the police pushed from her mind under the pressure of the unbearable pain. Unable to restrain herself, she pushed with every ounce of strength left, expelling the creature, the product of her dead lover's foul seed, onto the sodden, soiled bedding. She let her head fall back against the headboard and wept with relief, not bothering to tend to the newborn until she heard it's growling cries. She felt the sheets pull as the beast began to make its way toward her, and what must be claws pricked her gory thigh.

She leaned forward to collect her baby, but the gnarled umbilical cord hung, still attached, trailing up to disappear into her ruined vagina. Alice tugged to free it, and a burning pain flared inside her, as the stubborn placenta refused to be dislodged. Unable to get the scissors from the vanity drawer, she instead held the sinewy purple tether up to the thing's mouth, allowing it to gnaw through the cord with its tiny, sharp teeth.

Careful to avoid the biting mouth, she tenderly brushed his cheek, dislodging a maggot that had stuck there from the slime of the birth.

It was a boy.

THE HAND THAT FEEDS

"**H**EY, PAPA? WILL YOU tell us the story about when you were in prison again?" The boy rested his elbows on his knees, his eyes sparkling with mischief.

"Now, Bud, I wasn't *in* prison. I just worked there."

"Yeah, Papa. Tell us the story about when you and Nana worked at the prison." The girl set down the fashion magazine she had been flipping through and smiled. "It's my favorite."

"I don't know. Your mama doesn't like it when I tell that story."

"Mama's not here," the boy stated sensibly.

"What she doesn't know won't hurt her. We won't tell." The girl chimed in.

Papa leaned back in his chair and regarded his grandchildren with a look of playful consideration, bushy brows drawn together in thought and his lined face full of mock severity.

He knew he would tell them the story, but it was part of the game to draw it out a bit. It was tradition that the kids spent the last week of summer vacation with their grandparents ever since they started going to school, but he knew at ten and fourteen, they wouldn't want to hang out with their old grandfolks much longer.

"I suppose we have just enough time while Nana makes dinner. I could tell it one more time. So you want to hear about how me and Nana met and fell in love?" He teased, smiling when his grandson groaned.

"No, Papa. Tell us about Fatty!"

"It's *Frankie.*" The girl corrected her younger brother, earning a grimace that included both crossed eyes and a protruding tongue.

"That's right, sweetheart. It was Frankie." He grinned at his granddaughter before winking at her brother. "But he was a fatty."

Papa made a show of leaning back in his chair, one hand rubbing his gray-whiskered chin as he looked off into space and composed his thoughts. When it looked as though both children were ready to pounce upon the old man, fidgeting in their eagerness, he began the story.

***

"Frankie Hanson was as much a prisoner of his own body as he was of the State. A victim of his own insatiable appetite and a doting widow for a mother, he hadn't walked in over five years by the time he came to live at the state institution for the criminally insane. Now that's just a fancy name for a prison for crazy people, but we also took in the ones that had what they would call "special needs" these days. Frankie wasn't the first bedridden inmate I had ever dealt with. But at over seven hundred pounds (we weren't really sure because he had to be weighed on a shipping scale and we didn't have one of those) he was certainly the most memorable. Rumor has it that at the time of the murder he weighed around eight hundred, but he'd been on a special diet for several weeks before we got him, and he'd lost some weight. All I know is, he is still the biggest human being I've ever met.

"As I recall, it was quite a spectacle the day they brought Frankie in. I remember everyone who was able seemed to find a reason to be outside when the flatbed bearing the enormous, fleshy bulk of the new prisoner backed up to the doors of the loading dock. Before then, the dock's only purpose had been to receive machinery and food for the kitchen, but it was the only door on the facility that was big enough to bring Frankie in.

"It was late summer, so the weather was nice enough for Frankie to ride exposed to the air, and exposed he was. There weren't clothes big enough to fit him. Though his lower body was swaddled in massive sheets, he was otherwise naked, and I noticed that carloads of gawkers had followed him to the perimeter fence where they were prevented from coming closer.

"He sat upon a mattress that in turn sat on an extra-large shipping pallet like the kind they used in factories back then. I guess they still use them now, for all I know. It doesn't matter, anyways. An industrial forklift lifted his heavy ass off the truck and in through the doors, but after that, we were on our own.

"Now usually the inmates slept on standard bunks bolted to the walls, but there was no way this big bugger was going to fit on one of those. We ended up having to order a specially made hospital bed with a reinforced steel frame and some heavy-duty wheels that would allow us to move him around the prison. It took eight of us guards, and I mean *young, strong men*, an hour and forty minutes to shift ol' Frankie from that pallet to the bed, and let me tell you, there was *a lot* of groaning and cursing going on. But we got him there, and then three of us pushed him through the kitchen. I remember your Nana's pretty blue eyes were round as saucers when she saw him as we moved him across the building to where we housed the prisoners who, for some reason or another, couldn't be kept on death row at the state penitentiary. The whole time this went on, Frankie never said a word, nor did he even attempt to help us. He just stared straight ahead, his piggy eyes glaring at nothing and his thick bottom lip stuck out in a pout.

"Now, I don't have anything against heavy people, Lord knows I'm not as slender as I was in my youth. And I reckon some of them have cause to be the way they are. Ordinarily I might have had some sympathy for the man, it must've been miserable being as big as he was and bedridden and all. We housed some really bad men, all manner of murderers and psychos, but sometimes they were just so crazy you couldn't help but feel a bit sorry for them. But not Frankie. I knew the second I looked at his face he wasn't crazy. Oh no, that man wasn't crazy at all. Pouting on that bed was nothing more than a huge slab of selfishness mixed with a generous dose of meanness to boot.

"He wasn't crazy. He was just plain bad.

"Frankie was staying with us because he was just too big for death row. But that was where he belonged. Anyone who kills their own mama doesn't deserve to live.

"I didn't know the Hansons personally, but I knew the story. Father gone a month before Frankie was born, shot to death pursuing a robbery suspect. A good man and a good cop leaving behind a heartbroken wife and unborn son.

"I think in a way, it was probably Mrs. Hanson's doing that her boy turned out the way he did, but you can't blame a sweet woman like she was. She'd lost the man she loved with her body, so replaced it with loving her boy with food. Women used to take pride in cooking, but those days are just about gone. Hell, lots of women don't even know *how* to cook anymore. But then again, most men don't know how to fix a car, either, so I guess it's a wash.

"Now, there's lots of reasons a man might do bad things. Poverty, temper, craziness, or jealousy. But that wasn't the case with Frankie. In the end, he was just a child inside. I don't mean simple. I've known plenty of slow guys who do bad things. I remember one kid who got kicked in the head by a horse when we were teenagers who was never the same again.

"No, I don't mean Frankie was slow. He was as smart as the next man, but he was spoiled by his mama. A full grown brat was what he was. Just a selfish, horrible person.

"I guess his mama finally had enough of waiting on him hand and foot, so she decided she was going to put Frankie on a diet. There wasn't much he could do about it since he couldn't get out of bed, but she had tried before and always relented. This time she wasn't giving in. Frankie couldn't exercise on account of the fact he couldn't get up, but he spent a lot of time working his hands. Flexing and squeezing those little doodads they make to increase hand strength.

"The neighbors said they heard him bellowing for weeks on end, alternately pleading and cursing his mother. Begging for food and calling her all sorts of names when she didn't give in. Back then people didn't get involved in each other's business like they do now, so they turned a blind eye on the Hanson's house and tried their best to ignore it.

"Well, Frankie just kept getting madder about his mama withholding his food, and I guess one day they were arguing and she got too close. She wasn't a very big woman and he had those strong hands. He snapped her neck like an old, dry branch and things got pretty quiet after that. It was almost a week before the neighbors got concerned and called the cops, but by then he had her mostly eaten."

***

"Talk about biting the hand that feeds you, huh?" Papa winked and the kids groaned.

"Tell us about his leg, Papa." The boy begged, but Papa held up a hand.

"Who's telling this story, Bud?"

"You are."

"I'll get there."

"Just ignore him, Papa. I want to hear the rest." The girl glared at her brother before returning her attention back to her grandfather.

"Okay now. Where was I?"

***

"Working in the institution meant you had to get used to some nasty stuff on a fairly regular basis. It was just one of the things that came with the paycheck. You got used to it. You had to, or else you didn't make it very long. Anyone who lasted longer than six months was considered a lifer, though not many did. It wasn't boring, that's for sure. Sometimes it was quiet for a while, but it never lasted long.

"Full moons were the worst. Believe what you want about it,

but I can tell you for a fact that the moon affects people in strange ways. Anyone who's ever worked in a prison, bar, or hospital will tell you the same. Man, would those loons howl at the full moon. They went ape-shit. Anything that could happen, did. In fact, it was a full moon when the riot happened, but I'm getting ahead of myself.

"So we were used to gross things. Nutcases crapping on the floor, and then finger painting with it. Or jumping on their beds, playing with themselves like monkeys at the zoo, but it was nothing compared to Frankie. Not that Frankie could've played with himself . Even if he could've reached for it, there was no way he could find it. I know because we went looking for it one day while we were cleaning him. Damn thing was so buried in the pad of fat covering his groin it looks more like a belly button than a pecker.

"We were used to the crazy stuff and as used to the gross stuff as we could be, but nothing we had dealt with could've prepared us for Frankie.

"This was a long time ago before prisoners had much in the way of rights, and we were overpopulated and under-staffed. There weren't enough nurses to go around, so much of the day-to-day care fell to us guards. We were the ones who got stuck with making sure they got clean and didn't allow their wounds to fester. It wasn't such a big deal with most of them, a crazy man can take a shower and wash his own ass if you watch and remind him.

"But Frankie couldn't do anything for himself. Every few days we had to bathe him, a chore that took up to two hours and two guards. One of us would have to lift each fold of heavy flesh, while the other scrubbed out the cheesy accumulations of sweat that had collected and doused the area with baby powder to prevent chafing. If I live to a hundred, I don't think I will ever forget that smell. One time a bit of food got lost in all that fat and by the time we found it, maggots were teaming in the dark moistness. It was awful, but we did it just the same.

"Then there was the problem of the toilet. He couldn't walk, so he couldn't use one. That didn't bother Frankie one bit, though. He just did his business where he lay, not even trying to help us when we rolled him from side to side to change the bedding and wipe his huge ass. Sometimes he would hold it, waiting until one of us held up the massive apron of flesh that hung between his legs, and whizzing on the guard who was unlucky enough to have to wipe inside his folds. Whizzed right in my face one time and oh, how that big bastard laughed. Now, I'm not a violent man, but I sure could've killed him that day.

"Anyway, Frankie's legs were so fat, he had to keep them spread all the time, and he had these big, purple patches of growths on the calves. The skin there was as rough and pebbled as an old cobblestone path, splitting open and weeping a thick yellow fluid that constantly had to be wiped away. I know it pained him, but I couldn't bring myself to care too much. Not after he pissed in my face, anyway.

"Twice a day we would wipe the slime off, wash the crusty edges of the growths, and smear a thick salve over the entire area. Was kind of like rubbing Vaseline on a gator. Just touching his legs made my stomach churn. I came to hate Frankie like I've never hated anyone in my life. When the other inmates misbehaved, we shot them up with drugs or put them in solitary. But there wasn't much we could do to Frankie. We had to take care of him.

"The guards weren't the only ones who hated him. He wasn't there a day before the other inmates wanted him dead. It wasn't his disgusting nature that offended them. It was the noise. We had our fair share of wailers there, and the nights were few and far between when you couldn't hear the echo of someone sobbing himself to sleep or calling for his mother.

"But once again, Frankie was different. From the time he was secured in his cell that first day, he bellowed. Morning, noon and night it went on. *I'm starving! Feed me! Good God, I'm wasting away! Where's my food?* And so on. You could hear it no matter where you went, the cell block, the showers, even in the kitchen. The men we kept weren't compassionate on their best days, so it didn't take long for Frankie's whining to grate on already frazzled nerves. We had a kind of rapport with the prisoners. They acted up sometimes, but mostly we kept it under control. But Frankie's constant wailing riled the others, and unable to take it out on the actual object of their misery, they took it out on us. Work went from merely hard, to almost intolerable. I can't even blame them much. It was difficult for me to cope with, and I had all my faculties about me to begin with.

"After weeks of the commotion, we had all reached the end of our ropes. Like I said, this was back when prisoners were still treated like prisoners, not like now when they have more rights than I do. They didn't get pampered like they do now, and I'm not proud to say that guards could pretty much get away with whatever they wanted back then. I myself tried to always treat the inmates with dignity, but I knew plenty who didn't.

"I can't justify taking part in what we did to Frankie that day. I'm not even going to try, but I was awful tired, and just plain fed up with the man. It wasn't the right thing to do, but we did it anyway. And being sorry never undid anything.

"I'd been teamed up with another guard named Eddie something-or-other, his last name slips my mind, but we were partners when it came time to see to Frankie's needs. Eddie wasn't a bad man, but he had been dealing with the same crap I had for a lot more years than me, and it made him hard. Sometimes his idea of blowing off steam was to taunt the prisoners. I never condoned it, and had never participated until that day, but I never really held it against him, either. We weren't exactly running a daycare.

"So Eddie gets it into his head that we're going to screw with Frankie a bit and I go along with it, and we go to the kitchen and find the biggest, juiciest looking fried chicken leg they had. Then we went into Frankie's cell and showed him what we had. I swear that man burst into tears when he saw it, having lived on nothing but average-sized portions of the blandest, healthiest fare we could provide. He begged us for that chicken. Sobbed like a child and literally begged, his big face folding up as he blubbered, but

Eddie just held that meat up out of his reach and waved it around, making sure nothing but the smell got within Frankie's grasp.

"Well, Frankie had been losing weight, and I guess he thought maybe he had lost enough, or maybe he wasn't thinking at all. But I'll be damned if that big man didn't pull himself up from his bed. It took a long time and we both laughed at his struggling, but that stubborn fool got to his feet for the first time in five years.

"We weren't really sure what to do. I was a bit scared when I saw the look of triumph that lit up his face, but it faded the second he took his first step. Those legs of his weren't used to supporting *any* weight anymore, let alone his massive girth, and his shin bone split with a crack I can still hear, shooting out the front of his leg like a jagged, white sliver, all bloody and gooey on the inside. The worst part of it was—and just thinking about it makes me want to puke to this day—lumpy globs of fat splattered out of the torn skin and plopped on the floor. I heaved when I saw those yellow wads marbled with delicate red veins laying there on the gray tile.

"Frankie screamed and hit the floor, his leg still oozing fat and blood while Eddie and I ran for help. It took five of us over an hour to muscle him back into bed and push him to the infirmary, but by then he was unconscious from blood loss and shock. It was the first time he'd been quiet since he got there. I guess it nearly killed him, but no one ever asked why he had decided to stand in the first place. Eddie and I sure as hell weren't offering any details. They kept him for two weeks, and it was the most peaceful two weeks of my life. Even the other inmates seemed subdued, just enjoying the silence without Frankie. I think maybe it was the silence of his leaving that made them do what they did when he came back.

"The riot happened that Friday morning, maybe a week after Frankie returned to his cell and started his caterwauling again. It's a bit murky how it came about, but I can tell you those inmates held the institution for two whole days before they finally just gave in and got back in their cells. There wasn't much damage done and no one was badly hurt, but when all was said and done, Frankie was gone.

"There was some blood on the floor of his cell, but otherwise not a trace of the big man. The guys from the State came swooping in, trying to do an investigation, but no one was talking and they didn't have much science like DNA back then. To be honest, I don't think they really cared all that much. A lot of interviews were done, and photos taken, but in the end they really didn't try that hard. Frankie had no family left to complain, and his disappearance saved them the trouble of having to figure out how to execute him. They still used the electric chair in those days, and I'm sure those boys were sweating over how to fit that big tub of guts into it. Over the next few months, the prisoners were all transferred out to different institutions and the place was eventually closed, forcing all of us staff to look for other work."

***

"And that's the sad story of Frankie Hanson." Papa sat back, folded his hands across his stomach, and smiled widely, revealing his ill-fitting dentures.

"*Papa!*" the kids cried in unison.

"What?"

"You didn't finish the story. Tell us what really happened to Frankie." His grandson complained.

"And tell us the *truth* this time." His granddaughter agreed with her brother, a rare occurrence.

"Now there's a funny thing about the truth, sweetheart. Sometimes it has just as many layers as a lie. Papa always tells you kids the truth, but sometimes when we love someone, we have to decide which layer to peel. Cuz believe me, the truth can be much uglier than a lie."

"Please, Papa." The boy steepled his hands.

"Papa!" The girl was exasperated.

"Okay. I'll tell you the rest. But you have to remember, a lot of it is supposition. No one who really knows what happened during those two days has ever been willing to tell the facts."

***

"Now, I should probably backtrack a bit and remind you just how hard life was for everyone who had to deal with Frankie. I'm not trying to justify what may or may not have been done to the man, but sometimes a person can understand what drives others to do crazy things. Frankie was a pain in the ass from day one and none of us had a moment's peace from the time he came in except for when he was in the infirmary. Sometimes you can handle something until it stops, but after a reprieve, you can't handle it anymore when it starts up again. That's the way it was as soon as they took Frankie off the morphine and wheeled him back into his cell, and we all knew how bad it was going to get. Stress like that can make even a good man do bad things. A sane man can go crazy for just a minute. And let's face it; most who were involved had been crazy for years.

"But there's one more thing about Frankie you need to think about. It wasn't just hatred we all felt due to his annoying nature. It was also fear. The kind of deep-rooted fear no one ever even realizes they are feeling until after the fact. You see, that sloppy, fat-assed killer represented something within us all that terrifies us. The loss of control of our own bodies, and a lack of self-control over our desires and needs. I think we all know that way down inside us all is a Frankie, should we lose grip on the ability to control ourselves.

"What I'm about to tell you may all be just ugly rumors. But I'll tell you what most *believe* happened to Frankie Hanson during those two days, and you can do with it whatever you please.

"From the beginning, it was rumored the riot had to be a ruse, a set-up. One or more of the guards would've had to be involved for the inmates to all get free like that, with not even *one* escape attempt, but there wasn't anything anyone could prove afterwards.

"They got out that morning and took over the facility in a surprisingly organized way (which also leads one to think the guards were involved). The truth of the matter is, the State was never notified until *after* the situation was taken care of, which probably had something to do with why they closed us down.

"But you have to remember *everyone* hated Frankie, and maybe the inmates just did what the rest of us wanted to do, but were too constricted by morals to actually attempt.

"The story goes that they gathered together in the shower room and hatched a hasty plan, a few of the inmates left behind to hold off the guards in whatever way they did so. I'm not going to tell you how because the ex-guard in me doesn't want anyone to have that information. But after that, they went straight to Frankie's cell and got to work.

"If the story is true, the crazies stole sharp knives from the kitchen and each took turns poking him and making him squeal like a pig. This could've gone on for hours, if it's true, before he finally would have bled to death or died from the shock. That's when the tale gets truly disturbing.

"Rumor has it that one of the inmates had the idea to cut him all up, dress him out kind of like a deer? And they did just that, hacking away and lugging all of the pieces back to the kitchen. It would've taken a long time to do, he was such an enormous man, but they eventually got him chopped up and delivered. Now the same people who think the guards were part of it (depending on who you talk to, it was either *all* the guards, or just a few) also believe maybe a few of the cooks took part as well.

"So as it's told, those collaborators took what they were given and cooked up a mighty feast attended by the prisoners and staff alike. And they didn't leave the table until Frankie Hanson had been completely consumed along with some baby potatoes and garden fresh carrots. Then the prisoners returned to their cells and someone, maybe a cook or perhaps a guard, disposed of the bones. The State was called and all they found was some blood in a cell. Frankie Hanson was gone."

***

"Ewww Papa! That's so gross." The girl shuddered and grinned simultaneously.

"But I haven't told you the spookiest part yet." Papa leaned forward, his eyes wide with wicked glee. "Rumor has it some of those guards developed a taste for human flesh that day. You know there does seem to be an awful lot of people who go missing in the woods around town."

"Dinner time!" Nana stepped into the room, a stained apron around her waist and long strands of gray hair escaping the tight bun she wore at the nape of her neck.

"Yep, dear. We're on our way. Just have to get the kids to wash their hands." Papa stood up, his knees popping loudly and making both his grandchildren giggle.

"You kids get washed up. I'll be right in." Papa headed down the hall to the bedroom at the end, where he and Nana slept.

Closing the door softly behind him, he looked at the ancient trunk against the wall. It took only a minute to find the small, straight key that unlocked the heavy padlock on the front, and he eased the heavy lid open. The object he sought was towards the back, buried under material samples from when Nana had made her own wedding dress. He found it without effort, and carefully unwrapped the tattered velvet encasing it. A smile played on his lips, but never quite touched his eyes as he traced the smooth lines and contours, spending extra time on the ridges above the empty eye sockets, remembering the deep-set eyes. The yellowed skull felt cool under his hand, boiled clean of the flesh so many years ago.

"Papa?"

Papa pulled his hand back quickly, dropping the lid and clasping the padlock in place before turning towards the door. He could rewrap it when the kids were asleep.

"What is it, Bud?" Papa asked casually as he met his grandson at the door and the boy backed up a step so they were both in the hall. He snuck in close to his grandpa as they walked towards the sink.

"What do you think we, I mean *people*, taste like?"

"Well," said Papa with a wink, his voice low so as not to be overheard. "I suppose like Nana's meatloaf."

JACK AND JILL

JACK SAT AT THE worn kitchen table, his hands buried in the guts of an ancient radio, tinkering with the parts in a vain attempt to fix the antique. He told the owner, Mrs. Jones, that he feared the radio was beyond fixing, but she insisted with a clear statement that she *held complete faith in his abilities.* He mentioned how cheap it'd cost to replace nowadays, but she liked that one and would hear nothing of the new fangled junk they peddled at the ritzy stores in town. In the end, he let himself be brow beaten by an eighty-four year old woman who stood a foot and a half shorter than himself.

Though he mainly worked as a handy man around town, word of mouth brought him some additional side jobs when people started to realize his proficiency with small household electronics. It was difficult to find steady work, being an ex-con, so he happily accepted whatever odd jobs came his way. This one, however, proved more work than the twenty-five dollar fee was worth.

A scraping sound from the room above the kitchen drew his attention from his task.

She was moving around up there again.

He sighed and lit another cigarette, dragging deeply and rubbing his eyes as he exhaled a cloud of bluish smoke.

Too soon. He had nearly been caught the last time.

He turned his attention back to the project at hand, hoping that if he pretended not to hear her, she'd return to sleep, or whatever else she did up there. He no longer went upstairs.

He could smell her sickly sweet odor long before he heard the moist slap of her bare feet on the linoleum behind him. Jack sat up straight in his chair and stared directly ahead at the fading rose-patterned wallpaper, keeping his breaths shallow through his mouth to avoid the stench of decay. Only one thought went through his mind over and over again, like a dog chasing its tail.

Don't touch me. Please don't touch me.

Her gravelly voice made the hair on his arms stand up. "I'm hungry," she said.

"I know."

***

It was hard for Jack to remember what she looked like when she'd still been beautiful. He lost track of how much time passed since the nightmare began. In his mind, he pictured her while he slept, dreamt about how perfect the days went at first and how the nights flew by after they first met, back when he loved her.

He'd been hitchhiking from town to town searching for work to put food in his belly. The pickings were slim then. As soon as he exhausted all his resources in one town, he hitched to the next.

In this current town, more jobs than average presented themselves to him and he made enough extra money that he felt he deserved a beer for his efforts . . . despite the fact his parole officer might throw him right back in the penitentiary if he got caught. Of course, they'd have to find him first.

He wandered into the local watering hole and found himself a seat in a dark corner. Fresh out of the joint, he wasn't comfortable socializing with what he thought of as "regular" people.

Jack had been nursing the one beer he allowed himself— wishing it was Jack Daniels, though not quite trusting himself with whisky yet—when he noticed a pretty woman at the bar. She was staring in his direction.

He avoided eye contact, certain a woman that fine never intentionally looked at a man so average and unclean like himself. Yet when he dared a second glance, she hadn't turned away. Instead she smiled—at him.

The woman stood and walked slowly to his table. His palms began to sweat and he thought he might just slide off the chair and die from a nerve-induced heart-attack. She was so lovely and graceful. He couldn't pry his eyes loose from the sway of her hips.

Jack was hooked before she even spoke.

"What's your name, stranger?" she asked.

Her voice was even prettier than he imagined, and terrifying in that she actually used it to speak to *him*. Years had passed since he'd been next to a woman, let alone one so stunning. All the spit in his mouth seemed to dry up at once, leaving his tongue a thick, foreign appendage no longer his own.

"Um, Jack," he said, amazed he found the words at all.

She laughed, the look upon her face ripe with both mischief and promise. She held out her hand. "What a delightful coincidence. I'm Jill."

Not much later, Jill took him to her house in the country. They made love most of the night. For Jack it was unbelievable, the first sex he'd had in too many years. For him, she became an instant addiction. He would do anything to stay between her thighs back then.

Of course, that was before he knew what she was.

Hell, he still didn't know.

***

Jack stared out the windshield at the darkness of the highway, broken only by the glow of his headlights while he traveled south for the better part of two hours. His eyes felt full of grit. He'd gone too far already and decided to turn around at the next town to head for home.

Some nights proved successful; some, not. She'd make him go out again tomorrow. Absentmindedly, he fingered a deeply ridged scar on his left hand, a gift from Jill when he failed once before. He hoped she wouldn't get too angry this time. It wasn't as easy as it used to be. Now all of the rest stops were equipped with video surveillance.

After turning around to head north, Jack only drove about fifteen miles when his luck finally changed. Sometimes it went like that—once he was sure that the night's foray would be a bust, someone strolled across his path that suited her needs perfectly.

At times, he wondered if maybe she held some sort of power that stretched out from that old farmhouse to bend a man's will her way—but that was ridiculous, right?

The boy stood by the side of the road, his skinny shoulders covered by a lightweight jacket that was no match for the evening's chill.

At the sight of Jack's headlights, he stuck out his thumb, the universal sign for "How-about-a-ride, man?" Jack eased off the accelerator and gently braked to a stop half a block from the young man. He didn't want to seem too eager to pick him up. After a short jog to meet the car, the boy opened the passenger door, squinting at the dome light.

"Hey, can I catch a lift with ya?"

"How far you headed?" Jack asked. He motioned for the kid to sit down and close the door, which he did, tucking a dirty backpack between his feet on the floorboard. His shaggy bangs obscured most of his face and he twitched in a way that might've been nerves, though Jack suspected the tick was from some sort of chemical dependency. He'd seen his fair share of junkies in prison.

"Anywhere is good. Anywhere you can drop me." He rubbed his hands in front of the vent to warm them, though Jack thought it a ploy to hide how bad they shook. "Damn, its cold out there!"

Jack pulled onto the highway before he took the pack of smokes from his front pocket and lit one with a creased matchbook. The young man accepted one gratefully when it was offered and he settled a little more comfortably in his seat, opening the window a crack to ash.

In the back of his mind, Jack calculated when would be the

best time to grab the chloroform from under his seat.

"Only going about seventy miles up the road," he said through a cloud of bluish smoke. "There's a little town close by. Drop you there, if it suits you."

"Cool, man. Real cool."

***

Jack remembered his last victim, a scrawny girl, maybe seventeen or eighteen, definitely a prostitute. She had a certain hardness in her eyes that was uncommon in one so young. He recalled how nervous she immediately became upon entering the car and he wondered if maybe she smelled the slight chemical odor that always seemed to linger in the vehicle. Regardless of what initiated her unease, it didn't take very long for her worry to blossom into a full blown panic.

She mentioned that she might have made a mistake asking for a ride, but he ignored her. Eventually she got the courage to tell him to pull over and let her out. When he still didn't respond, she began to plead. She got so fidgety, he worried she might just open the door and jump out, regardless of the pavement racing by at sixty miles per hour, so he locked the doors.

And while he was debating what to do with her, that's when he glanced in his mirror to see the flashing lights of a state trooper.

Jack slowly pulled to the gravel shoulder of the road.

Aw shit! The cop would search the vehicle and find the chloroform, find the rope. Finally coming to an end now. He saw himself again in the joint, maybe in a padded cell this time. This was it.

The odd part was how much the thought of prison seemed to calm him. Maybe going back wouldn't be so bad. He was tired of this game. Probably time that he should get caught . . . but then what would happen to Jill?

The girl sat beside him with wide, apprehensive eyes. If she seemed nervous before, she was positively petrified now. Taking the opportunity to speak before the officer made it from the patrol car to Jack's window, he leaned slightly toward the girl and spoke in a flat whisper near her ear. "It's illegal to hitchhike in this state."

The girl said nothing, just continued to stare at him with her wild blue eyes. He was gambling on the fact that the girl might be more afraid of the cops than of him.

As it turned out, the gamble paid off. She might have had an outstanding warrant for her arrest. She definitely carried some drugs. He found a little baggie of pot in her rear pocket when he disposed of her clothes later that evening. Whatever made her keep her mouth shut, he was thankful.

He had a short in one of his taillights, the cop told him. The pig gave him a fix-it ticket. And that was it . . . not noticing the odor of chloroform that Jack was sure poured out of the car; no interest in the girl in the passenger seat, other than to quickly pass the flashlight over her head and nod a greeting. Jack drove away with a grim smile on his face and stuffed the ticket in his glove box.

"Dude, you wouldn't happen to have any weed on ya? Some pills? Anything, man. I'm in need of a little something right now. Help a brother out?"

The boy's voice startled Jack out of his thoughts, banishing the scenario with the dead girl from his mind. Without looking at him, he nodded once.

Seconds later, he wasn't terribly surprised to feel the boy's hand creep into his lap.

He continued to drive without reaction but the young man shyly fumbled with his zipper until he slipped his hand into the front of Jack's boxers.

Jack wasn't gay, but in prison sometimes companionship became more important than gender. It'd be easy to just pull over, forget his original intent, and let himself be distracted by the friction of the kid's warm, slightly damp hand on his own rising flesh.

It had been an awful long time since sex with Jill was an option. Oh, he was pretty sure it could still be done—plenty of gooey places existed on her body where he might stick it in. To do that, though, he'd probably have to look at her. Definitely have to touch her. Worse yet, she might actually touch him.

Jack shuddered slightly at the thought, and was surprised to realize that the kid actually got a reaction from him. He gently removed the boy's hand from his crotch with more regret than he cared to admit. A time and place for everything in life, and this was neither. He had a job to do . . . a job that was nearly at an end.

"Not here." Jack said. "We'll be at my place soon. I have all kinds of good stuff there. It'll be a real party."

"Cool," the kid said with a grin. Jack returned his smile. Maybe he wouldn't need the chloroform at all this time.

***

When he pulled up to the long driveway, Jack felt a pang of conscience that was entirely alien to him. These acts never really bothered him before. The risk that the hunt posed did, but he'd never felt any sympathy for the young people he delivered to their deaths. He wasn't the sort that wallowed in such a useless emotion as guilt.

Jack quickly tried to squash the feeling under what he felt was a valid excuse. The young man was obviously strung out on drugs. That road only ran in two directions: overdose or prison. He didn't know how painful it felt to die with a needle in your arm, though he saw firsthand what the other inmates did with a tender young thing like his new friend—and that wasn't a life worth living.

He did the kid a favor by bringing him here.

Jack opened the door and held it so the boy could enter first, then turned and locked it behind them. If the boy thought anything strange, he didn't mention it, and only stepped aside while Jack headed to the end table where he stashed the drugs, parting gifts from former passengers.

"What the fuck is that smell?" the boy asked. His voice finally showed a hint of anxiety.

Jack turned, meaning to make something up about a dead raccoon in the attic, but he stopped short when he saw the kid's calculated smile. The boy held a gun, leveled at Jack's face.

"Give me the drugs and all your money, you old pervert." The kid's tone became all business. This was definitely not his first rodeo. "I'll be taking your piece of shit car, too."

Jack stood stunned, unable to yet grasp the quick turnaround. This time he'd been the one set-up.

"I said give me the shit!" The young man shoved him hard with the heel of his free hand.

Jack fell onto the sofa. The boy was certainly stronger than he guessed. Of course, he wouldn't be strong enough.

He heard Jill moving on the second floor. Jack had intended to do the young man a favor by getting him high before she came down, but it seemed Jill wasn't in the mood to wait. For once he was gracious, though not thankful enough to want to catch sight of her.

Jack closed his eyes tight as he heard her moist tread on the stairs and smelled the full assault of the sweet, rank odor that preceded her. The boy made a face when he must've smelled her too, though he never comprehended what was coming until her hands found his neck.

After that there was only screaming. There must not have been any bullets in the boy's gun, Jack thought, after waiting for the absent shots. Jack took the opportunity to head into the kitchen, his eyes cast upon the floor so he wouldn't see more than her feet. They were bad enough—black and swollen, rivulets of yellowish fluid weeping from skin stretched so tight it looked shiny, about to burst.

Jack made it to the kitchen counter and stood there, his back to the door, his right hand automatically reaching for the bottle of Jack Daniels he kept there. He took a long pull, trying to block the horrible scene out, and his hands trembled while he lit a cigarette. The screaming he got used to easily enough, but not her smell . . . not her nauseating, pungent reek.

That, and the liquid sounds of her feeding.

He squeezed his eyes shut and chugged the whisky. His cigarette burned down to his fingers, but he barely noticed, dropping it in the sink without opening his eyes. He remained there, unwilling to move, through the entire horror, and when it was over, he stayed there still, until he was certain she went upstairs to settle into her cloying room. Only after he was absolutely sure she wouldn't come back down did he move to survey the damage and start the gruesome task of cleaning up whatever bits and pieces Jill left behind.

***

Jack sat at the table again, the radio fixed and whole, ready to return to the spot on Mrs. Jones's windowsill where she listened to it while washing her dishes. He stared at the radio without really seeing it, lost in his own mind, caught on too many questions that he couldn't answer. Questions that scared the hell out of him.

Things were so much different than they'd been at first. Jill no longer came downstairs at all unless she needed him, though she seemed to need him more often every week. He always doubted that Jill was her real name and patted himself on the back for being quick enough to realize she probably chose the name just to be cute. Now he seriously wondered if she was even human.

Summer was coming; her smell would only get worse. No amount of air freshener held a chance in hell to mask it. He wondered how much longer she, *they*, could go on like this.

Maybe she was dying. Maybe she'd been dead when they met.

Jack took a shot of whiskey, this time from a shot glass rather than straight from the bottle, and glanced out the window, his eyes resting on the little shed outside. Inside sat an unused lawnmower, a weed whacker, gardening tools . . . a gas can. He was pretty sure it was still full.

He knew what he should do with that gas can, but he lit a smoke instead and stared out the window some more, trying to turn his thoughts elsewhere, into his fantasies.

Long-legged, nude beauties danced through his imagination while he kissed those young nymphs on all of their pink parts . . .

But that escape soured as well. Lately his fantasies grew

darker until he didn't want to dream anymore either.

Again he looked out at the shed.

He knew what he should do, what he needed to do. It wouldn't even be that difficult. Take that gas can, splash it around, strike a match, and run like hell. Then go wherever he wanted. Never look back. Drink until he scoured the memories from his brain or damn well died trying.

He knew it'd never work that way. There would be an investigation. Someone would get curious. Maybe they'd poke through that unusual looking compost heap behind the shed, find the bones. He'd be hunted. They'd find him too, he never doubted that.

No, that wouldn't be the way to do it. If he wanted out, there on the floor sat the boy's empty gun. Before he lit the match, he'd buy a bullet, just one, because he knew exactly where to put it, and blow his brains out while the world burned around him.

Bang! All over for both of them—

The footsteps he'd missed while lost in his thoughts now stopped behind his chair. Jack heard what passed for breathing just over his shoulder.

If she touches me, I'll do it! I swear to God I will!

"I'm hungry," she said.

"I know."

CPSIA information can be obtained at www.ICGtesting.com
Printed in the USA
BVOW061251070312

284610BV00004B/4/P